Miss de Bourgh's

Adventure

a sequel to Jane Austen's

<u>Pride & Prejudice</u>

by

Joan Ellen Delman

Acknowledgments:

Many thanks to my friends & readers at the Republic of Pemberley, with special thanks to Rae for so much helpful information about Bath. Warm thanks also to the fabulous Ms. Ariel of arielcollage.com for her beautiful cover design.

Miss de Bourgh's Adventure : ISBN 1-4116-4647-9

www.janeaustensequels.com

Chapter 1

The Reverend William Collins, who, through the affability and condescension of Lady Catherine de Bourgh, held the living of Hunsford—and who deemed it his duty, on that account, to offer to his great patroness those little delicate compliments which are always acceptable to ladies— had more than once remarked to her ladyship that her charming daughter seemed born to be a duchess; that the most elevated rank, instead of giving her consequence, would be adorned by her; and that Miss de Bourgh's indifferent state of health, by preventing her being in London, had deprived the British court of its brightest ornament.

Such sentiments as these were frequently, and most eloquently expressed by Mr Collins. And Lady Catherine herself declared that, in point of true beauty, Anne was far superior to the handsomest of her sex, because there was that in her features which marked the young woman of distinguished birth. But if the truth were told, Miss Anne de Bourgh was thought by many to be rather plain. Not so hideously plain as to frighten small children, but plain nonetheless: thin and small and pale; with a timid air, and insignificant features. Having said so much, it seems unnecessary to add anything more by way of a description. A young woman without beauty, however estimable in character, can have no attributes worth naming—no thoughts worth revealing—and certainly no business being heroine of a novel. One thing further, nevertheless, might be said of Miss de Bourgh: she was heiress to a great fortune, and to very extensive property; and it was very well that she should be. If a lady cannot be beautiful, she ought at least to be rich.

Miss de Bourgh's father, Sir Lewis de Bourgh, was long deceased; and she had, for many years past, lived in retirement with her mother, Lady Catherine de Bourgh, and her companion and former governess, Mrs Jenkinson, at Rosings Park, the family estate in Kent. She was believed by all and sundry (herself included) to be constitutionally delicate, with a strong tendency to ill-health; and doubtless, in comparison to her mother, whose extraordinary vigour was a matter almost of legend amongst her acquaintance, Anne was somewhat deficient in vital energies. Yet it must be owned that her perpetual weakness and languor were perhaps owing more to mental fatigue and lowness of spirits, than to any real physical debility.

Like many another young lady of large fortune, Miss de Bourgh might have found great pleasure in having the power to do as she liked; but to do as she liked had never been in her power. She had lived her life under the sharp eye, firm hand, and commanding tongue of her respected mother; and had exercised as little authority over the course of her own life as may well be imagined. Had Sir Lewis de Bourgh lived, or had her ladyship been blessed with a large family of children, Anne might have been able sometimes to escape her mother's harassing superintendence. Most unhappily, however, Anne de Bourgh was Lady Catherine's only child.

Like most mothers, Lady Catherine desired to see her child well disposed of in marriage. Towards that end, she had, from their infancy, intended a marriage between her nephew, Mr Darcy, and her daughter; and Anne herself was not averse to the idea of marrying her handsome cousin, if the gentleman were willing. But alas! Mr Darcy had never shown the smallest inclination for the match; and he had, in the end, disappointed Anne, and outraged her mother, by marrying Miss Elizabeth Bennet—a young woman without family, fortune, or connections—in spite of all Lady Catherine could do or say to prevent him. Her ladyship exerted to the full all her celebrated sincerity and frankness of character in the effort, thoroughly abusing Miss Bennet to her face, and to Mr Darcy as well; but to no avail.

After a little time, however, Lady Catherine rallied, and concocted another plan: she had a second nephew, Colonel Fitzwilliam; *he* would marry Anne. It was not so good a match as the first. The Colonel, though the son of an Earl, was but a younger son, with only a small fortune at his command. Still, it was in every other way a most eligible connection, and her ladyship again employed all her faculties to see it accomplished. But poor Lady Catherine was most unfortunate in her nephews. Colonel Fitzwilliam, too, chose to marry elsewhere; and Anne seemed doomed to a future of elegant spinsterhood, ruled by her mother, and with no other friend to sympathize in her cares than old Mrs Jenkinson, her paid companion.

Anne sometimes thought she might have found a friend in Mrs Collins. Charlotte Collins was about her own age, and on the whole, a kind, and an exceedingly sensible young woman; but she had one defect too serious to be overlooked. To Anne's astonishment (for despite the gallant compliments he was wont to lavish on her, Anne could not but consider Mr Collins a very disagreeable gentleman), Mrs Collins appeared quite oblivious to her husband's prosing stupidity. To be married to a man so idiotic, so irksome as William Collins, and yet to look upon him with a bland indifference—to never betray any feeling of disgust or annoyance in his society, was a degree of sense, or of insensibility, which Anne could neither understand nor respect. So, though she saw Mrs Collins tolerably often (for the Collinses dined twice each week at Rosings; and Anne, when taking the air in her phaeton with Mrs Jenkinson, frequently stopped just outside the garden gate of Hunsford Parsonage to speak to her, though she was scarcely ever prevailed on to get out), no real intimacy had ever arisen between them.

Thus, at the dangerous age of nine-and-twenty, and despite the sumptuousness of her surroundings, and the possession of every luxury in the way of gowns, jewels, servants, and carriages which heart could desire, Miss Anne de Bourgh's prospects for future happiness looked exceedingly bleak.

But if adventure and romance will not find a young lady at home, she must leave her home to seek them. Lady Catherine, almost despairing of a worthy candidate presenting himself at Rosings in the foreseeable future (for she had quite exhausted her supply of eligible nephews), was yet determined on finding a princely consort for her noble daughter. Accordingly, she seized upon a little lingering cough of Anne's as a pretext for carrying her to Bath, and introducing her at last to that aristocratic society which she had been formed so manifestly to grace. Indeed, where better than Bath, her ladyship reflected, to make new acquaintance, and to renew old? She congratulated herself upon the shrewdness of the plan, and set about at once to accomplish it.

Within a week's time, a superior house in Sydney Place had been taken in their behalf, and Lady Catherine and Miss de Bourgh, accompanied by Mrs Jenkinson, and Dawson, her ladyship's maid—and with a proper number of postilions and outriders to attend them on their journey—set forth from Rosings with every appointment that comfort or luxury could require.

Lady Catherine talked almost without pause until they reached the first stop of their journey, Mrs Jenkinson taking advantage of a few very brief silences to enquire whether Miss de Bourgh was quite warm enough—to ask whether she would like the glass let down a little, or put up entirely—to rearrange her cushions—to offer her refreshment—and to express a fear that she was indisposed.

"When we get to Bath, Anne," said Lady Catherine, "you must go into the warm bath every morning before breakfast. Mrs Jenkinson" (nodding at that lady) "will attend you. I recommend also that you will continue with your regimen of Holt's Elixir*, one dose morning and evening; and by these means, your cough will soon be cured entirely. I shall take you myself to Madame Le Clerc for new gowns; for you have had nothing new this season, except the half-dozen morning gowns from Mrs Leland—and those I do not regard as anything; the work of a mere country seamstress, not fit to be seen away from home. Madame Le Clerc is the best modiste in Bath, and you may be sure will be *au courant* with the very latest fashions. When your dresses are ready, we will begin by visiting the Pump Room in the afternoons, where perhaps we may find we have some prior acquaintance. In any event, I will be able to survey the Book, and see who is arrived. I make no doubt we will meet with many who are known to me from one place or another, and we shall have no difficulty situating you in a sphere befitting your rank and fortune. However, I think you had best not attend the Assembly; your health will not allow it. You are far too delicate for dancing—which is most unfortunate, indeed. Had your health permitted you ever to learn, your proficiency would certainly have been far superior to the common, for you possess that natural grace characteristic in those of aristocratic descent. I am confident you would have danced delightfully. But, as I was saying—to sit about in the hot, stuffy Rooms all night, would be altogether too much for you. And some of the less exalted persons who may be met with at such a public gathering you would scarce be equal to encounter. You have not been used to keep such company; and I would advise you not to hazard it. You will find more than enough of such society at the Pump Room, where at least you may benefit from drinking the waters; and once we have established you in the proper circle, of course, you will be able to accept invitations for the occasional private dinner or card party, where the company is to be confined to a select few, and which will therefore be sufficiently elegant, and quiet enough not to overpower you."

Her ladyship continued on these themes for some time, and when they were disposed of, found no shortage of other subjects upon which to discourse. They changed horses at Bromley, came through London in their way, and stayed overnight at Reading; and by leaving very early in the morning, reached Bath the following evening in time for supper.

With considerable agitation had Anne set out from Rosings, and with greater still did she alight at Bath. Her life had been always so confined — she had mixed so little in society — that she was at once apprehensive and elated in the prospect of new acquaintance and new experience. Though her own ill-health had been given as the reason for this trip, Anne was aware her mother had another motive for the visit; and she felt much in doubt as to what would be its final outcome. She dreamt of forming an attachment such as she had read about in novels; of escaping her mother's tyranny by marrying a handsome and tender gentleman, who would treat her with affection and kindness, and devote himself to fulfilling her every wish. But at times she thought it more likely that (as also frequently happened in novels) she would be deceived — misled — taken in; would find herself the defenseless prey of a devious and heartless man, who only wanted her for her fortune, and whose baseness and cruelty would make her regret Lady Catherine's milder sovereignty. Or (perhaps worse still!) she might excite the interest of no man whatever; and be obliged in the end to return home to Rosings, an abject figure of failure and disgrace.

All that lay before her was uncertain in the extreme; but Anne endeavoured, as nearly she could, to hope for the best.

Chapter 2

Lady Catherine and her daughter were soon settled in their new quarters, their linen, plate, and other necessities having been sent on to Bath ahead of them, and all having been made ready for them before they arrived. At first, Anne found little more to enliven her at Sydney Place than she had found at Rosings Park. As her mother commanded, she went into the warm bath attended by Mrs Jenkinson, and saw scarcely anyone but gouty old men and rheumatic old women. She went dutifully to the modiste and the milliner with Lady Catherine, where she was fitted for a profusion of gowns, pelisses, bonnets, spencers, shawls, and other attire, all of her ladyship's choosing, and therefore with more of ostentatious richness, and less of real elegance, than Anne herself would have preferred. And she submitted to the prescribed regimen of Holt's Elixir, though with rebellion in her heart, and queasiness in her stomach, at each repeated dosing.

At last, however, her new finery was ready, and Anne was ushered with all due solemnity into the Pump Room, Lady Catherine on one side, and Mrs Jenkinson on the other. Her ladyship found them acceptable seats, and then walked off to inspect the Book. As Anne took the glass of water proffered by Mrs Jenkinson, she noticed a young lady and gentleman, both very elegant and both very handsome, standing nearby. Gazing on them with admiration, she raised the glass to her lips and swallowed a large mouthful of water. With a cough and a splutter, she gave forth an exclamation of disgust, and screwed up her features in a manner hardly consistent with dignity, but indicative of the strongest distaste. The elegant young lady caught her eye and smiled in sympathy.

"It is rather vile stuff, is it not?" the young lady ventured to say.

"But my dear Louisa!" said the young gentleman. "How could it be otherwise? Do you suppose the precious gift of health is to be acquired without suffering for it? Can you regard with favour the paltry influence of nourishing food and drink—of fresh air and sunshine—of wholesome amusement—of restorative sleep—beside the bracing effects of foul tinctures, nauseous nostrums, and poison pellets? Would you hold at naught all the accumulated wisdom of that honourable profession, which would bleed and purge and poison us to death, to cure us of our maladies?"

The young lady laughed at her companion and abused him as ridiculous; and Anne, thinking of the hated Elixir, could not but smile. Before anything further could be said, however, Lady Catherine returned from her perusal of the Book.

"I find, my dear," said she, "that Bath is by no means full as yet; it is still a little early, however. In another fortnight we shall find a great deal more society than is here at present. But I believe I *have* seen the name of one dear friend, whom I knew long ago, before I married Sir Lewis de Bourgh. Mrs Arabella Wynnewood is listed as letting a house in the South Parade—a respectable address—with Mr George Wynnewood and Miss Louisa Wynnewood. Mrs Wynnewood can be none other than my old friend, Miss Hatfield, who married a gentleman by that name. The Hatfields are of noble descent: Miss Hatfield's uncle was the eighth Baron Hatfield. And Mr Wynnewood (like your own father) was the representative of an ancient and illustrious, though untitled line—and possessed of a very large property. They will be a most suitable family for you to associate with, Anne; though whether the Mr Wynnewood whose name is inscribed in the register be husband or son, I know not."

This speech, delivered with Lady Catherine's customary authoritative resonance, was overheard by the handsome young gentleman, who was at that moment standing alone, his female companion having just gone off to talk with another acquaintance. He stepped closer and said, "Mr Wynnewood I believe is the lady's son, ma'am."

Lady Catherine turned to stare at him, amazed at his impertinence. She did not wish to cut him entirely, however, lest he should prove to be someone worth knowing. After a moment's hesitation, she asked in her coldest and most stately tone,

"You are acquainted with the family, are you, sir?"

The young man, not the least intimidated by her ladyship's imposing demeanour, replied with perfect equanimity, "Intimately, ma'am. Indeed, I am in a position to satisfy you particularly on this point. I spoke with Mrs Wynnewood only an hour ago. The gentleman you were so kind as to make mention of *is* her son; and though I am sorry to have to perform so unpleasant an office, I feel I must just drop a little hint of caution to you, that you may not be taken entirely by surprise. You will find the young man but a boorish fellow, I am afraid—quite a clown. Of course, I need not enlighten you as to the excellency of *Mrs* Wynnewood's character, since she is already known to you. And with *Miss* Wynnewood, I will not hesitate to assure you, you will be perfectly delighted—should you choose to pursue the association, that is."

"Thank you, sir," she said dismissively, turning away. She opened her mouth to say something further to Anne, when to her unmatched astonishment the young man spoke again.

"But after all, why should dread of the boorish brother hinder you from making the young lady's acquaintance? Here comes Miss Wynnewood now—will you allow me to introduce her to you? But I beg your pardon; I must first introduce myself. Mr George Wynnewood, at your service."

He swept her ladyship a very low bow, and ended it with a quite audacious little wink at Anne; who no doubt ought to have been highly affronted at his impudence, but was instead so bewitched by his good looks, and so flattered by his notice, as to see nothing but perfection in his manners. Even Lady Catherine, though far more worldly and more scrupulous than her daughter was, could not but be affected by Mr Wynnewood's manly beauty—which, it must be owned, was far beyond the common. He was, besides, the son of her old friend, and a gentleman of very fine family. Who could say but that he might not do very well for Anne?

"Upon my word," she declared, "you are a very pert young man! But your mother, as I recollect, was not without her ebullitions of vivacity; I suppose you have inherited her wit. And so, that young lady is your sister, is she? I am Lady Catherine de Bourgh; this is my daughter, Miss de Bourgh."

The young ladies curtsied at each other, and Mr Wynnewood bowed again, first to her ladyship, and then to Anne. Lady Catherine thereupon deigned to hope his mother was well, and began to question him: Was his father living?—Had he any more sisters or brothers?—Where was their home?—When had they arrived in Bath?—What had brought them there?—How long did they intend to stay?

When at length she paused in expectation of an answer, he addressed her with respect, but with none of that awe she was accustomed to receive.

"My mother," he said, "has been a widow these twelve years past, your ladyship; I am her only son, and Louisa her only daughter. We three are come to Bath solely for the winter pleasures, as we are all so fortunate as to be in excellent health. Abbey Chase (the estate in Cumberland which I inherited from my excellent father) is a grand place —comprising a fine old mansion and extensive park, with a large pleasure grounds; and surrounded by a lovely countryside—with every charm which that implies, to be enjoyed in the milder seasons; but it is somewhat dark and forlorn in the colder part of the year. For my sister's sake, and for my own, my dear mother determined this year on our spending the winter in a more lively spot, where we might find some congenial society to cheer us; and all of us being agreed in preferring Bath to London, we made the journey a fortnight ago yesterday, and are now quite comfortably settled in a house at the South Parade."

He then listened most attentively as Lady Catherine began to speak of herself and, to Anne's discomfiture, of her daughter—Rosings Park—Sir Lewis de Bourgh—her brother, the Earl of _____—her nephew, the master of Pemberley—Miss de Bourgh's delicate health—Miss de Bourgh's education—Miss de Bourgh's good taste and refinement—&c., &c.

Whilst her ladyship extolled Miss de Bourgh's virtues to Mr Wynnewood, Miss Wynnewood (perhaps taking pity on Miss de Bourgh's embarrassment) engaged Anne in a friendly conversation. Anne felt her kindness; and they talked a little of Bath, and of other topics, until Lady Catherine announced to Anne that they would accompany Miss Wynnewood and her brother back to the South Parade, that she might lose no time in being reunited with her old friend.

They all walked out together, Lady Catherine giving instructions to Mrs Jenkinson, who was to run a few errands for her whilst they paid their call—and who previously had been all but forgotten, by both Anne and herself, in their pleasure at meeting with Mr and Miss Wynnewood. When they reached Lady Catherine's waiting carriage, she asked where their own carriage was.

"Our coachman is an exceedingly leisured fellow, your ladyship," said Mr Wynnewood, "and our horses the most pampered creatures on earth; for my sister and I are in the habit of walking everywhere, and scarcely ever bother with the carriage."

"My mother, ma'am," explained Miss Wynnewood, "has often lectured us on the wholesomeness of the exercise, and its benefit to the health; and even she herself, when she goes out, most often goes on foot. We always walk a great deal when we are in the country; and though we find ourselves now in town, have yet to relinquish the habit."

"Your mother is indeed correct," affirmed her ladyship. "Walking is a most healthful exercise; and, would her health permit her to undertake it, I should certainly recommend it to Miss de Bourgh as a very salutary activity. But it is, unfortunately, much beyond her strength; she would find such an exertion entirely too fatiguing. I am sure, however, you will both consent to accompany us in the carriage."

They acquiesced most graciously; but Anne was conscious of a little feeling of resentment in her heart towards her mother. She could not deny that she was easily fatigued; but why must Lady Catherine be forever publishing her debility? If she really wished to see her daughter well-married, was it not impolitic to dwell so upon her weakness to every acquaintance? Was it possible any gentleman worth having would wish to wed so feeble a creature as her mother continually represented her to be?

Lady Catherine's footman was hard by, and ready to help the ladies into the carriage, but Mr Wynnewood superseded him. He offered his hand first to Lady Catherine, who declined his assistance, indicating that she had some final orders to communicate to Mrs Jenkinson before they departed. After handing the two young ladies into the carriage, he climbed in himself; and it suddenly occurred to Anne that, not only were the Wynnewoods without a carriage, but they had also no servant attending them.

"Do not you have a maid or footman to accompany you when you are out, Miss Wynnewood?" she asked.

"Ah!" said Mr Wynnewood. "Our country habits betray us again, Louisa. We relish our independence, Miss de Bourgh, and when we go out, we dislike to be hampered, either in our movements, or in our conversation, by the presence of a servant. Instead, I myself serve as my sister's footman and chaperon; for I am so favourably impressed with my own strength and skill at pugilism (the only field of study in which I excelled at Cambridge), as to think myself an adequate protector of her person, and of her honour, too."

"How very singular," cried Anne, envying them the freedom they enjoyed, and the companionship they found in each other. *Perhaps it would have been so for me,* she reflected, *had I had a brother.*

"Your strength and skill indeed, George!" Miss Wynnewood exclaimed. "Is he not an abominable coxcomb, Miss de Bourgh?"

"Oh! no—not at all."

"My sister speaks the truth, Miss de Bourgh. I am quite a bad character altogether, and you ought to have nothing to do with me. I tremble to think what might become of you, if you were to spend much time in my company—though, for myself, I confess, I can think of nothing more delightful."

"Oh!" she replied with a blush.

Mr Wynnewood looked back at her with a smile which caused her to blush more deeply still, and look away. He really was quite the handsomest man she had ever seen—a good deal handsomer even than her cousin, Mr Darcy! She was thinking these thoughts, and looking out the carriage window to hide her confusion, when, in a kind of odd detachment, she saw Lady Catherine striding purposefully across the street, and heard the sound of a carriage, driven very fast*, clattering over the cobblestones. There was a yell, and a shriek, and an awful crunching and cracking; and the next thing she knew, her mother lay lifeless before her eyes, broken and bleeding in the middle of the pavement!

Chapter 3

"I know not how it happened, Miss de Bourgh!" sob-
bed Mrs Jenkinson. "Her ladyship was in the midst of ex-
plaining to me about the errands she wished me to undertake for her, when her notice was attracted by something—I
know not what—across the street. 'It is not to be borne!'
cried she—and before I had any idea what she intended, she
had dashed out into the street and—and—"

Mrs Jenkinson dissolved into tears, and could say no
more. The truth was that Lady Catherine, as she stood on
the sidewalk conferring with the old governess, had espied
a young couple across the street (lower servants, by the look
of them, or perhaps tradespeople) flirting shamelessly, for
all the world to see! And when the young man grew so bold
as to actually kiss the brazen little hussy, in plain view of every passerby on that very public thoroughfare, Lady Catherine had felt it incumbent upon herself to go and scold the
culprits into decorum. Unfortunately, she was so intent on
her mission that she neglected to look about her before
stepping into the street—assuming, perhaps, that no mere
coachman would have the temerity to run down Lady Catherine de Bourgh—with the tragic result we have already
described.

Mrs Jenkinson had been reduced nearly to hysteria by
the calamity; but Anne herself was strangely calm. It was
quickly ascertained at the scene of the accident that Lady
Catherine was not dead; and with the greatest possible care,
she had been transported back to Sydney Place. Mr Nichols,
a most capable surgeon, who had been fetched with all

requisite haste, was now examining Lady Catherine in her bedchamber. Anne sat in the drawing room with her two new friends, and the tearful Mrs Jenkinson, awaiting his opinion of the case.

"I hope you will believe, Miss de Bourgh," cried Mrs Jenkinson, "that if there was anything I could have done to prevent her ladyship from—from—. But it was all over be‐fore—before—"

"Dear Mrs Jenkinson—you mustn't think that anyone blames you," said Anne. "I know how determined my mo‐ther can be, when once she sets her mind on anything. You could not have hindered her from doing what she would."

At last they heard footsteps on the stair, and shortly afterward, Mr Nichols entered the room.

"Your mother is a woman, Miss de Bourgh," he told Anne, "of most remarkable fortitude. She has sustained inju‐ries which would have killed anyone with an ordinary con‐stitution. There are several broken bones, along with many cuts and bruises; and I suspect some injury to the head as well. Nonetheless, I believe her ladyship will, in time, make a full recovery. I have left her for the moment in the care of her maid, who is, I think, a competent person to sit with her for now; but with your permission, I will engage a couple of skilled nurses to attend her ladyship night and day. She must not be left alone."

"Of course, sir," said Anne. "Please make whatever arrangements you think necessary. Is my mother suffering a great deal?"

"No; she is not sensible at present, though she did twice regain consciousness, briefly, whilst I was setting the bones. When she does waken, she will require laudanum to dull the pain of her injuries. I must warn you, also, that her recovery is likely to be very slow; she will be confined to an invalid's couch perhaps for many, many weeks. The warm bath, though, when she is strong enough to be conveyed into it, should be very helpful to her convalescence."

"Ought I to go up and see her now?" asked Anne.

"I leave that entirely to you, ma'am; certainly it can do her no harm, in her present state. I imagine you are anxious to see her, but if she wakens, take care that you do not tire her, and that she is not agitated in any way. I will take my leave now, Miss de Bourgh, and send the nurses to you as soon as may be; and I shall return again in a few hours' time, to see how her ladyship progresses. Until then, of course, you will send for me if I am needed—though I do not anticipate any change for the worse this afternoon."

"I thank you, sir, for all your assistance. Mrs Jenkinson, will you see Mr Nichols out, please?"

When they had left the room, Miss Wynnewood took Anne's hand very kindly, and Mr Wynnewood said, "We too, I suppose, ought to take our leave, Miss de Bourgh; and I trust you will understand that we should never have intruded ourselves upon you at such a time, save with the hope that we might be of some comfort or help to you."

"Oh! yes—thank you—thank you both. Your presence here today has indeed been of very great comfort to me; so much so that, I own, I am loath to part with you—Miss Wynnewood," she concluded hastily.

"Nor can I think it right," said that young lady, "that you should go through such a trial alone, Miss de Bourgh; and I should be glad, very glad to stay with you, for as long as I can be of service. But I am a stranger to you; and I cannot but think you may prefer the companionship of persons more familiar to you. You have Mrs Jenkinson, of course; but is there no other friend you might send for, to stay with you while your mother is indisposed?"

Anne deliberated for a moment. "No. I can think of no one. There really is no one at all—except—perhaps—Mr Collins."

"Mr Collins?" said Mr Wynnewood with a glance at his sister.

"Mr Collins is the vicar of our parish; he and his wife, and their little boy, live just across the lane from Rosings Park, at Hunsford Parsonage, and are frequent visitors at

Rosings. To be perfectly honest, I do not feel a very great regard for Mr Collins; but my mother has rather a partiality for him."

"Oh, do send for him, then, Miss de Bourgh," said Miss Wynnewood. "Surely her ladyship would benefit from the advice of her spiritual counselor, in facing the lengthy recuperation which lies ahead."

Despite the gravity of the situation, Anne could hardly suppress a momentary smile at the notion of Lady Catherine de Bourgh taking advice from anyone, let alone Mr Collins —whose great aim in life, so far as she could tell, was to agree with every word his patroness uttered. She had not the smallest wish to see Mr Collins in Bath; but she must think of what was best for her mother. Lady Catherine, when she awoke, might in fact find some odd sort of comfort in Mr Collins' attendance; and in truth, she herself would not object to having Mrs Collins at hand to assist her. She felt herself quite unequal to the demands of overseeing the household management, Lady Catherine having always had such matters wholly under her own control. Mrs Jenkinson, Anne readily foresaw, would be of little help under the circumstances, and Dawson must needs devote all her attention to her mistress. But Charlotte Collins—so capable, so practical as she was! Charlotte Collins would understand exactly what was required.

She expressed these thoughts to her new friends; and, with a little further urging from Miss Wynnewood, she at length resolved on having a letter dispatched to Mrs Collins to apprise her of what had happened, and to suggest that she and Mr Collins might be of use to Lady Catherine and herself, if they would see fit to come to Bath. This having been decided on, and the writing of the letter undertaken by Mrs Jenkinson, Mr Wynnewood again suggested that he and his sister ought to take their leave; but the steadfast Miss Wynnewood would on no account abandon her new friend.

"You must go, I think, George. My mother will be

wondering what has become of us. But," (again taking Anne's hand most kindly), "I myself shall stay with Miss de Bourgh, for as long as she wishes."

"Very well, Louisa. I own, I shall be happier to think of Miss de Bourgh, knowing she is in your company. At what o'clock shall I come back for you? Or shall I send the carriage round this evening?"

Miss Wynnewood hesitated. "I hardly know. Perhaps, if Miss de Bourgh would be so kind—perhaps Miss de Bourgh would be so good as to send me home in her own carriage? And then, my dear friend, I may stay until you find yourself quite thoroughly weary of me."

Anne of course declared it impossible such a circumstance could ever come to pass; but she assured Miss Wynnewood that the carriage should be at her disposal, whenever she might wish to avail herself of it.

Chapter 4

One evening, not many days after Lady Catherine's accident, Mr Collins and his wife entered the drawing room at Sydney Place. Anne had scarcely an opportunity to welcome them before the clergyman rushed at her and seized both her hands, imprisoning them between his own damp palms.

"My dear Miss de Bourgh!" cried he, "Mrs Collins and I are come in the greatest haste, to support and console you in your present affliction! We departed Hunsford almost at the very moment, I may say, in which we received the awful tidings from Mrs Jenkinson. To think of that noble spirit, laid low by so grievous an accident! It is almost enough to shake one's faith in the Almighty Himself! Great indeed must be your suffering, my dear Miss de Bourgh, under the weight of this heavy misfortune. But," he added after a moment's pause, looking down at her with a watery gaze in which were mingled a fulsome pity and a repellent servility, "we must not give in to despondency under this cruel blow. Her ladyship is strong; and we, too, must be strong, for her sake. Lady Catherine de Bourgh will not sink under this trial. Of that there can be not the smallest doubt! And you, my dear Miss de Bourgh—you are your mother's own daughter. You possess within you that same noble and resolute spirit—though your delicate health has ever prevented you from displaying it."

Anne, not wishing to be uncivil, yet disconcerted both by Mr Collins' proximity, and by his obsequious sympathy, faintly stammered out some conventional phrases of gratitude, in which the words "obliged," "regret," and "imposition" were just barely audible.

"Imposition!" exclaimed Mr Collins. "My dear Miss de Bourgh—! If I could but begin to convey to you the deep and profound sense of honour, felt both by Mrs Collins and myself, when we understood you had chosen to turn to *us* in your hour of need! Indeed, if our humble presence here can be of the smallest possible service to you or to her ladyship in this bleakest of times, it will be a privilege beyond description!"

Anne murmured a few more incoherent acknowledgments, and Mr Collins at last released her from his grasp. She was then able to give her attention to Mrs Collins, who had been standing by in silence during the whole of her husband's oration. Anne thanked her also—with a little more of warmth than she had been able to muster for Mr Collins—and begged them both to be seated.

"What is Lady Catherine's present condition, Miss de Bourgh?" Charlotte Collins enquired. "Is she at all improved since Mrs Jenkinson wrote to us?"

The surgeon had seen Lady Catherine but a short while earlier, and Anne went over for them everything he had told her afterward. They briefly discussed his opinion, which was still very optimistic; and Mr Collins was just entering on another fulsome speech when Anne exclaimed,

"But Mrs Collins, where is dear little William? Surely you did not leave him behind at Hunsford?"

"We stopped briefly in Hertfordshire, in our way here," said Charlotte, "and left Willy with his grandparents at Lucas Lodge. Mr Collins felt we ought not to bring him with us to Bath."

"Oh! I am very sorry indeed to hear it. He is such a sweet little boy—I should have been pleased to have him in the house. I ought to have instructed Mrs Jenkinson to make mention of it, when she wrote you."

"My dear Miss de Bourgh!" cried Mr Collins. "You are all affability and condescension—so like your esteemed parent! And I do assure you, I have the very highest possible opinion of your wisdom, in all matters within the scope of your understanding; but permit me to say that, as a clergyman, I flatter myself I have had a good deal more experience of illness and injury, than such an elegant and prosperous young lady as yourself—which is of course only right and natural. What, indeed, should Miss Anne de Bourgh, daughter of the right honourable Lady Catherine de Bourgh, and the heiress of Rosings Park, have to do with the putrid contagions of the sickroom, or the wretched misery of the lame and crippled? Such afflictions belong to the sphere of the clergyman. It is as peculiarly his duty to see to them, as to the setting of his tithes; the composition and delivery of his sermons; the christening, marrying, and burying of his parishioners; the care and improvement of his dwelling; and the cultivation of attentive and conciliatory manners, especially towards those to whom he owes his preferment, and anybody connected with them. And devotedly attached as I am to my little olive branch, I hope you will permit me respectfully to submit, my dear Miss de Bourgh, that the noise and commotion of an exuberant little boy would by no means be agreeable, in the abode of suffering and sorrow."

Anne hardly knew what to say in response to this effusion, and only smiled weakly. She was much relieved when Mrs Collins proposed to her husband that he might go up and see Lady Catherine then, to furnish her with what comfort he could. At her suggestion, Mr Collins started up, offering to Miss de Bourgh his profuse apologies, that he had neglected to go up at once; and all impatience to dispel, by every means in his power, the agonies of his venerable patroness.

When he was gone, led upstairs by Mrs Jenkinson, Mrs Collins said, "Lady Catherine's accident must have caused you great anxiety, Miss de Bourgh."

"Yes," said Anne. "That is—not so much at first, somehow, as I would have expected. But later, when I went up to her room after the surgeon had gone, it was indeed a shock. To see my mother—who has been always so power-ful, always so much in command of everything and every-body—lying there helpless and insensible! I believe I should have been altogether overcome by the sight, had it not been for Louisa."

"Louisa?"

"Miss Wynnewood, I mean." Anne went on to explain how she and Lady Catherine had met Miss Wynnewood and her brother at the Pump Room; that they were the son and daughter of Lady Catherine's old friend, and that both had been present when the accident occurred.

"They came back with me to Sydney Place, and were very kind and encouraging while we awaited the surgeon's opinion. It was Miss Wynnewood who suggested I ought to send for you and Mr Collins. She felt I ought not to be alone at such a time."

"She sounds like a sensible young lady, and an atten-tive friend. Have you seen her again, since that day?"

"Oh! yes. She and Mr Wynnewood—with Mrs Wyn-newood, too—have visited every day since the accident. And since my mother regained consciousness, Mrs Wynne-wood has been sitting upstairs in her room, sometimes for long intervals, reading to her, and amusing her in any manner she could think of, whilst Louisa and Mr Wynne-wood have been keeping me most agreeably occupied downstairs. My mother is very weak now, and, I believe, really grateful for Mrs Wynnewood's attendance. They have been such a comfort to us both, Mrs Collins! It feels as though we had been intimately acquainted for years. In-deed, Miss Wynnewood and I are already addressing each other by our Christian names—have been doing so, for two days now."

"How fortunate that you should have met with such kind friends, at such a difficult time," said Charlotte. "I hope I may have an opportunity to meet them soon."

"You will meet them tomorrow, most likely. Miss Wynnewood and her mother promised they would call in the morning. I daresay they will spend a good part of the day here; and I cannot but think that Mr Wynnewood will come with them."

Anne was not mistaken in her assurance. Mrs Wynnewood and both her children called at Sydney Place the next day, a little after noon. They were accompanied by another gentleman, a naval officer by the name of Turner, who was introduced to Anne and Mrs Collins as a childhood friend of Mr Wynnewood's. They had known each other as boys, Mr Wynnewood explained, but before meeting that morning at Barratt's, in Bond Street, had not seen each other in fifteen years. Captain Turner, finding himself at liberty during the present peace, had come to Bath seeking relief for an injury received more than a year earlier, which had never been entirely healed, and from which, at times, he still suffered considerable pain.

The Captain, it must be owned, did not appear to advantage by the side of his good-looking friend. He was a very gentlemanlike man, but rather quiet and sober, and not at all handsome. He and Mr Wynnewood were the same age; but Captain Turner had lived a good deal in his thirty-one years, more than half of them at sea, and looked much the older of the two.

Mrs Wynnewood expressed a desire to see Lady Catherine; and Mr Collins being at that moment upstairs with his patroness, Anne felt it right that she should bring Mrs Wynnewood up herself, and introduce her to that gentleman, if Mrs Collins would be so good as to perform the duties of hostess in her absence. When she came down again, she was accompanied by Mr Collins, who had been for the moment dismissed by her ladyship, in preference to the society of Mrs Wynnewood.

During Anne's brief absence, Louisa and her brother had been discussing with Captain Turner and Mrs Collins a plan, just formed between them that morning (the day being unseasonably fair), to venture across to the Sydney Gardens, and take a stroll by the canal. They now proposed to Anne that she and the captain and themselves should make up a little walking party; and with the greatest civility invited the Collinses to join them as well.

"I am by no means ill-disposed," said Mr Collins, "to join in a party of this kind, in the company of respectable young persons such as yourselves. Though Mrs Collins and I have come to Bath for the sole purpose of assisting Lady Catherine in her recovery, whilst that noble lady is so ably entertained by your estimable mother, sir," (nodding at Mr Wynnewood), "I think there can be no objection to our taking a brief respite, for the sake of such healthful exercise and wholesome recreation as an outing of this description must provide. And no doubt the presence of Mrs Collins and myself, as chaperons to your charming little party, should help to allay any fears her ladyship might feel, as to her daughter's partaking in it."

Though having felt the greatest inclination for the expedition only a moment earlier, Anne now anticipated that her pleasure in it would be considerably diminished by the addition of Mr Collins. She was again most opportunely rescued by the intervention of Mrs Collins, who hinted to her husband that she and Mrs Jenkinson would be adequate to the task of chaperoning Miss de Bourgh in a walk with her friends; and that Lady Catherine, though at present occupied with Mrs Wynnewood, might at any time require Mr Collins' attendance, and certainly would not be pleased to find he had gone out. Such a line of reasoning was to Mr Collins unanswerable; and after another lengthy discourse on the duties of a clergyman, he graciously allowed the party to depart without him.

Once outside, Mr Wynnewood offered his arm to Anne, who took it most happily. Captain Turner followed behind with Miss Wynnewood; and bringing up the rear as they entered the Gardens were Mrs Collins and Mrs Jenkinson. They strolled unhurriedly until they reached the canal. Crossing one of the lovely bridges which spanned it, they all paused to survey the scene. It was too early in the year for flowers, or for any of the elegant amusements which would abound later in the season; nor was there even much greenery in evidence. Nonetheless, there was a decided charm to be found, both in the soft mildness of the air, and in the serene, unadorned beauty of the bare trees and the still water; and Anne, who had had seen little of nature save what could be observed from a window at Rosings Park, was enchanted with this closer view.

When they resumed their walking, there was a little change: Louisa, less than captivated, perhaps, by her companion's solemn demeanour, walked quickly on ahead of her friends. The Captain, undeterred, kept pace with her; and the pair soon outstripped the others by a few hundred yards.

"Poor Turner," said Mr Wynnewood to Anne in a confidential tone as they proceeded along the footpath. "He hardly cuts a dashing figure, does he? I believe he is already quite smitten with Louisa, poor devil! But the sorry truth is, he has scarcely two shillings to rub together. His father was a sort of gentleman-pauper, you see, and cannot have left him anything to speak of — except a widowed mother and a spinster sister to support as well as he can. And he told me he was posted Captain only a few weeks before the peace was declared, so he cannot have had a chance at much prize money as yet. He is lodging in a couple of cheap rooms in Westgate Buildings. But there is no harm in him; on the contrary. He is an exceedingly good fellow, I believe. He needs cheering badly; so I hope you will not take it amiss, Miss de Bourgh, if you find yourself sometimes in his society."

"Oh! no," said Anne, much struck by his kind intentions toward his friend. "Not at all. He seems a very — good sort of person. But do you really think him in love with Miss Wynnewood? They have only just met, after all."

"It happens too often to be a matter of any surprise; Louisa has always one gentleman or another trailing after her. I cannot think poor Turner has much chance of succeeding with her; but who can predict? Sometimes girls like a plain, awkward fellow like that."

"And if your sister did like the captain, Mr Wynne-wood—could you allow her to marry a man with no fortune?"

"Why, as to that, if she loved him, I suppose I should not object to the match. I think it wrong to marry, except for love. Don't you, Miss de Bourgh?"

Anne could not immediately look up at his handsome face as she murmured a few words of accord, but she felt a powerful thrill in her breast. Was he speaking only of Louisa and Captain Turner? Or had his question a more personal significance? At length she gathered the courage to meet his gaze, and was rewarded with a dazzling smile which did nothing to quiet the tumult within her.

After a little pause, he said, "I can afford to make Louisa a handsome settlement, you know, if need be; and indeed I would, if she chose Turner—he truly is a good fellow. But I very much doubt it will come to that. How quickly she walks! It does not promise well for my friend's chances."

Anne could hardly blame Louisa, who was so beautiful herself, if she were indifferent to Captain Turner. No doubt she could do much better than an impoverished, ill-favoured naval officer. At the same time, Anne could not but feel some sympathy for the captain, who really did seem a worthy gentleman, so far as she could tell; certainly his friend thought him so. These sombre reflections soon led to more agreeable ones: of Mr Wynnewood's remarkable kindness to his old friend—of his generosity and disinterestedness in the whole affair—and of his laudable inclination to marry only for love.

Chapter 5

With Lady Catherine confined to her bed, and suffering considerable pain from her injuries, Anne was almost
ashamed to acknowledge to herself how greatly she enjoyed
this little outing. Yet so much pleasure did she take in the
beauty of the Gardens, and in the delights of Mr Wynnewood's society, that, when at length they returned home,
she was astonished to find she had been walking nearer two
hours than one, and with hardly any feeling of fatigue. As
the Wynnewoods were preparing to take their leave later
that day, Mr Wynnewood suggested that, if the weather
continued fine, they should all ride over on horseback the
following day to Charlcombe, or Claverton—or perhaps up
to Beechen Cliff, whence they might obtain a panoramic
view of Bath and all the surrounding countryside.

"That would be lovely indeed, Mr Wynnewood," said
Anne. "But I am afraid I—I do not ride."

"Not ride!" said he. "You are teazing me now, Miss de
Bourgh! A young lady like yourself, not ride—impossible! I
am sure you are an accomplished horsewoman."

"No—truly, Mr Wynnewood!—I am not. My father
did teach me to ride when I was a little girl; but it is a very
long time since I have been on a horse. I was advised to give
up riding many years ago, because—because it was thought
not good for me."

"Miss de Bourgh's health, you see," explained Mrs
Jenkinson, "has been always rather delicate, sir; she has
been ordered to avoid any needless exertion."

"But my dear Mrs Jenkinson!" said he. "A woman so knowledgeable and judicious as I know you to be—why, surely you must be aware what a wholesome exercise riding is."

"Indeed," Mrs Wynnewood attested, "I know of nothing so beneficial, nothing so likely to impart strength to a weak constitution, as riding. Would not you agree, ma'am?" she said to Mrs Collins.

"I have often heard it spoken of as a healthful exercise," Charlotte owned.

"I never feel half so well myself," said Louisa, "as when I ride every day."

"There! And I doubt not," said Mr Wynnewood, appealing to Captain Turner, "my good friend the captain will say the same."

"If you did feel inclined to try it this once, Miss de Bourgh," said Captain Turner, "I should not think it could do you any great harm."

"And really, Miss de Bourgh," added Mrs Wynnewood, "I must confess that you look perfectly hale to me. I see no sign whatever of weakness or frailty in you."

"Perhaps," said Mr Wynnewood with a smile, "you have been suffering merely from *ennui*—a most debilitating condition, with which Louisa and I were all too familiar before we came to Bath."

What young lady could long hold out against such inducements as these? Thinking of their walk today—of the great pleasure it had given her, and how little it had tired her—Anne began to feel that perhaps she might be able to ride after all. All of them, save Mrs Jenkinson, seemed to think it perfectly reasonable that she should, and she was almost persuaded herself.

"But even if I wished to go," she said, thinking aloud, "I have no horse, and no habit."

"A pity!" said Mr Wynnewood, still smiling in the most bewitching manner. "And of course, in such a desolated outpost as Bath, there can be no place to hire a horse."

"Nor any dressmaker between here and London," said Louisa, also smiling charmingly, "who might outfit you with a habit."

Anne soon yielded to their joint urging. The Wynne-woods had an engagement that evening in Camden Place, they said, and could stay no longer; but before they left, it was decided (over the gentle protests of Mrs Jenkinson) that Anne would go to the modiste's that very afternoon to obtain a habit; and, weather permitting, George and Louisa Wynnewood would come back the following morning at eleven o'clock for their ride. Captain Turner, as he was obliged to hire a horse for his own use, was entrusted with the commission of procuring one for Miss de Bourgh as well.

When her guests had departed, Anne ordered the carriage to take her to Milsom Street without delay. Mrs Collins was to accompany her on the errand. As they waited for the carriage to be brought round, Mrs Jenkinson endeavoured to dissuade Anne from pursuing such an imprudent course as she was now embarked upon.

"My dear Miss de Bourgh," the old woman importuned, "should you not at least consult your mother, before taking such a step? I am persuaded Lady Catherine would not approve."

At this Mrs Collins, seeing Anne's uneasiness, spoke up.

"I cannot think there is any necessity to trouble her ladyship over so trifling a matter, Mrs Jenkinson," she said. "Miss de Bourgh doubtless means to exercise every caution tomorrow; and the Wynnewoods and Captain Turner I am sure may be relied upon to see that she comes to no injury. To impart your concerns to Lady Catherine would cause her needless anxiety — which you must allow is to be avoided at all costs, in her present state. And — I believe it will be best not to mention the matter to Mr Collins, either. My husband might feel himself bound to inform Lady Catherine, and thus undo all the precautions we are taking — for her ladyship's sake."

"Dear Mrs Jenkinson," Anne added, "You are good to worry about me; but I do promise to be very careful. And I do so wish to go!"

Mrs Jenkinson could say no more. The carriage was at the door, and Anne and Mrs Collins hastily departed.

Though expressing some surprise at seeing 'Mam'-selle' without her mother, Madame Le Clerc welcomed her as warmly as might be expected, given that the young lady had already proved herself a most valuable customer. She had great hopes that Miss de Bourgh's patronage would help to revive, amongst the fashionable, the fading prestige of her establishment.

"If you will be so good as to peruse the books and select a pattern, Miss de Bourgh, I will have my assistant bring out some fabrics for your consideration. I am sure we can find something charming for you; and whatever you choose, I think I may promise to have your habit for you by Tuesday."

"Tuesday!" exclaimed Anne. "But I was hoping to have it for tomorrow morning, Madame."

"Tomorrow! *Bon Dieu* – it is impossible, mam'selle. Monday, perhaps –"

"Could you not keep your girls working a little later tonight? I do not mind what it costs."

A little glow kindled in Madame's eyes. "Stay a moment, Miss de Bourgh – I do believe I have just the thing for you. It was made for another lady, but she – eh – she left town before we completed it. It will need only a few alterations, I think, to fit you beautifully."

She sounded a little bell, and a young woman appeared in the doorway.

"Dorine," Madame commanded her, "bring in the blue velvet riding habit we made for Mam'selle Morton."

"The blue velvet, Madame? But Miss Morton –"

"Dorine!"

Madame seized her assistant and hurried her out of

the salon. Mrs Collins, listening to the muffled voices of the two women talking in the next room, and more wise in the ways of the world than her companion, concluded that the unfortunate Miss Morton had not in fact left Bath at all, but nonetheless would have to go without her habit for a few days more. She was about to whisper her suspicions to Miss de Bourgh, but a moment's reflection caused her to think better of it. If Anne understood what the modiste intended, no doubt she would insist upon the habit's being kept for the person who had ordered it. But after all, Charlotte reasoned, could Miss Morton's need for the garment be half so great as Miss de Bourgh's? Anne de Bourgh had lived all her life under her mother's governance; she had waited years for this chance at a little innocent amusement. Miss Morton—whoever she might be—surely could wait a few days longer for hers.

The habit was brought in directly, and when Anne put it on, Madame Le Clerc said, "Ah! It looks splendid on you, mam'selle. *Très splendide!* Just a tuck here, and there, and *voilà!*—perfection."

"What do you think, Mrs Collins?" asked Anne.

"I think it becomes you very well, Miss de Bourgh," Charlotte replied with perfect sincerity. "The dark blue colour suits your complexion; and the cut shows your slender figure to advantage."

Anne smiled. "It is a very pretty style, is it not?" To Madame Le Clerc, she said, "I like it very well, Madame. But will you be able to finish the alterations in time?"

"It will be delivered to you by ten o'clock tomorrow, Miss de Bourgh," she promised.

Anne retired to bed later that evening, in happy contemplation of the future which seemed opening before her. At the same time, she was really quite frightened at her own audacity. Never in her life had she done anything without the prior approval of Lady Catherine; yet she now intended not only to act without that approval, but to do precisely what Lady Catherine would have forbidden her to do, had she known of it. She strengthened her resolve with the thought that, however much her mother might object to her intention of riding, she certainly could have no objection to Mr Wynnewood, the wealthy and well-born son of her old friend, as a companion, or even (dare she think it?) as a suitor for her daughter's affections. Allowing herself in fancy to paint the brightest possible picture of George Wynnewood's growing attachment, Anne forgot to listen for the chiming of the hall clock downstairs; and she knew not what time it was, when at last she drifted off into a deep and untroubled slumber, graced by the sweetest of dreams.

She awoke early in the morning, however, with a stiff, aching feeling in her limbs, owing to the unaccustomed exertion of the previous day's walk. At first she feared she would have no choice but to give up the day's outing after all; but on finding herself breakfasting alone with Mrs Collins (for Mrs Jenkinson, feeling herself a little unwell, was still abed, and Mr Collins had gone out on an errand), Anne confided her trouble to the clergyman's wife. Mrs Collins, after a little deliberation, suggested that a visit to the warm bath might afford her some relief, and offered to attend her there if she wished to try its efficacy. It was still quite early, and there would be ample time to try what the waters could do, and be back in Sydney Place before the Wynnewoods arrived.

The two ladies finished their meal and left directly. Anne had not gone into the hot bath since her mother's accident, but this morning she submitted to it most willingly; and so efficacious did the measure prove that, once they were back inside the carriage, Anne could hardly express her gratitude warmly enough to Mrs Collins, for proposing it. As they drove back down Stall Street, her spirits rose; and she looked out the window with the keenest interest in every sight which met her gaze.

The carriage was stopped for a minute on Cheap Street, and Anne, peering down a narrow lane off to one side of them, espied a gentleman who looked very much like Captain Turner, in close conversation with an extremely shabby-looking older man.

"Look, Mrs Collins!" she exclaimed. "Is not that Captain Turner?"

Mrs Collins looked. "Yes," said she. "I believe it is."

"I wonder who that man with the wooden leg can be? He does not look at all respectable. Good heavens! The Captain is giving him money!"

Anne was silent a moment, thinking of what Mr Wynnewood had said about Captain Turner; and of certain novels she had read, wherein a trusting heroine signs a bill for a friend, and embroils herself in all manner of difficulties thereby—or an unsuspecting gentleman is lured into high play, and falls into the hands of unscrupulous creditors as a result.

"You don't suppose he could be a moneylender?" she asked her companion. "Someone to whom Captain Turner is in debt? Mr Wynnewood said he was very poor."

"Did he?" said Mrs Collins. She mused silently for a few moments, before adding, "But I hardly think your conjecture can be right, Miss de Bourgh. However poor Captain Turner may be, that other man looks a good deal poorer—he could never have had anything to lend, I think. More likely he is a beggar, and the captain is merely giving him a few pence, out of charity."

"Of course; it must be as you say," Anne agreed as the carriage moved on, and the two men were lost to their view. Mrs Collins' explanation made perfect sense, and she tried to be satisfied it was so. She could not bear to think poor Captain Turner might be in desperate circumstances, and yet feel too proud to ask his old friend for aid.

Chapter 6

Madame Le Clerc was true to her promise, and the blue velvet habit was delivered to Sydney Place not long after Anne and Mrs Collins returned from the bath. Captain Turner also was punctual to his appointment, leading a second horse alongside his own just before eleven o'clock. Anne had been watching for her friends from the drawing room window, and hastened out at once to greet him.

"Good morning, Captain," she called to him as she walked out. She descended the steps to make a closer inspection of the horse he had hired for her use. It was of a pale wheaten colour, with faultless contours, and ideally suited to carry a woman.

"What a beautiful animal!" she exclaimed. "I am exceedingly grateful to you, Captain Turner, for taking so much trouble on yourself."

He quickly dismounted, and made her a little bow. "The trouble was very little, I assure you, Miss de Bourgh," said he. "I am glad you approve my choice."

"I am no judge of horses," she admitted, "but I would not suppose there could be two opinions on the superiority of this one." She stroked the mare appreciatively. "But I am surprised. I should not have thought an officer of His Majesty's Navy would know anything about horses."

"We have not much to do with them, it is true; but I had the advantage over many of my fellow officers, in possessing an uncle with a very fine stable. I used to stay with him every summer when I was a child, and I learned a good deal about horses through his instruction."

There was a brief pause then, and Anne looked up the street. "I wonder what can be keeping Miss Wynnewood and her brother?" said she. "They are usually so prompt."

"I am a little early, I think," said Captain Turner, adding with a smile, "but your eagerness to be riding perhaps makes the wait seem long. If you like, we might ride up and down the road here for a bit, until they come. That way, you will have an opportunity to become used to the horse."

"Oh! yes—I should like that very much."

By so readily acceding to the captain's proposal, Anne recklessly tossed away the chance of having George Wynnewood to assist her into the saddle; to instruct her in the proper way to sit; and to take her hands in his for a few moments, for the purpose of mending her faulty management of the reins. But though it was only "an ill-favoured naval officer," and not the handsome Mr Wynnewood who performed these offices for her, she nonetheless found the performance not wholly disagreeable. The day was lovely; it was exciting to be riding once again, after an interruption of so many years' duration; and Captain Turner, if not so captivating a companion as his friend, was at least perfectly amiable.

As they slowly rode, side by side, up Sydney Place, Anne, by way of making conversation, remarked, "Mr Wynnewood said you and he knew each other when you were boys. Did you grow up in the same parish?"

"In a manner of speaking," he replied. "My father was a private tutor, and George Wynnewood was one of his pupils. He lived in our home for several years."

"And the two of you were good friends?"

"Very good friends. But I went into the Navy at fourteen, and (except during one short visit home a couple of years afterward) I have not seen him since. The next time I was in England on leave, he had completed his private education, and was gone off to Cambridge."

"Your father being a scholar, Captain, I wonder what can have made you choose the Navy as your profession?"

"My family home is on the south coast, near Portsmouth; and is it not foreordained," he asked with a twinkle in his eye, "that every boy who grows up near water should be desperate to go to sea?"

She smiled. It was much easier to talk to him than she would have supposed. "And have you any brothers who were similarly — stricken?"

"Apparently not," he replied, laughing. "I have only one brother, who is a scholar, like my father, and a clergyman; and four sisters, three of them married. Caroline, the youngest, still lives at home with my mother; she is just eighteen."

"I am an only child myself. I have often wondered what it would be like to have brothers and sisters."

"It is decidedly agreeable. Except when it is — not."

She smiled again.

"I believe Mr Wynnewood mentioned your mother was widowed, Captain Turner?" she asked after a slight pause.

"Yes. My father passed away several years ago; but I was at sea when he died. I was summoned home as soon as he was taken ill, but I arrived only in time to attend his funeral."

"How sad! But it must have been a great comfort to your family, that you could be with them at such a time."

After another little silence, he said, "You lost your own father some years ago, did you not, Miss de Bourgh? You said it was he who taught you to ride?"

"He did. My father died when I was but twelve. He was a gentle and a — a very kind man. I miss him still."

Captain Turner nodded in sympathy, and another, longer silence ensued. They had by this time made a few passes up and down the street, and at length the captain asked,

"How are you enjoying your ride so far, Miss de Bourgh? Now that you have had more time to form an opinion, do you still find the mare to your satisfaction?"

"Oh! yes. She has not the smallest fault that I can perceive. Indeed, I can think of nothing I have done which has given me greater pleasure, since—oh, in a very long time."

He seemed gratified by her response, and they turned again at the end of the street and rode back in the opposite direction. Anne really thought him a very agreeable gentleman, and felt now more than ever anxious to know that he was not in any sort of money difficulties; and she hardly stopped to consider what she was saying, before she blurted out,

"Mrs Collins and I saw you this morning, Captain, as we were coming back from the baths."

"Did you?"

"We were on Cheap Street, and I saw you down a little alley. You were speaking with someone who—who had a wooden leg."

"Ah! You saw me, Miss de Bourgh, with a man I have known as long as I have been at sea—Gower is his name. We served on three ships together; when I first had command of the *Amphitrite*, he was my coxswain. An excellent man, and a first-rate sailor in his day. How much he taught me, when I first came aboard the *Defiance*! But he was discharged from service two years ago when he lost his leg, and I had heard nothing of him until I ran into him on the street this morning."

Anne knew it was shockingly impertinent in her to be enquiring into his private affairs; but (she could not help acknowledging to herself with a wry inward laugh), was she not the daughter of Lady Catherine de Bourgh? And with such an inheritance, was she to be kept from finding out whatever she was determined to know, by a fear of being impertinent?

"I hope you will forgive my mentioning it, Captain, but I also saw—I saw you giving him some money."

The Captain looked rather abashed. "It was but a trifling sum." Then under his breath, he added, "Would to God it had been more!"

This last remark was made as a vent to his feelings, and not intended for Anne to hear; but she heard it nonetheless.

"Is your friend in some trouble?" she asked.

He hesitated before replying, "I am afraid he is, Miss de Bourgh. He can get no work, and his wife is very ill. They are altogether in the most wretched of circumstances."

"But many people are cured of all sorts of conditions by the waters here, are they not? I understand there is even a hospital, for those who have not the means to procure private treatment. Why does not his wife go there?"

"They did in fact come to Bath in hopes of having her admitted to the hospital. Unluckily, they were in ignorance as to the required procedure: they had not had the necessary letters sent from their parish before they came, nor received prior authorisation from the hospital. Nor did they have anything like the three pounds needed for caution money."

"Caution money?"

"To ensure that patients have the means to return home when their treatment is completed—or to pay for their burial, if need be. The money is most often provided by the home parish, or by a wealthy benefactor; but the Gowers knew nothing of these requirements until they arrived here."

"No more did I!—But three pounds is a small sum."

"For some, it may be; but for my friends, it is a fortune."

She grew thoughtful as he continued, "So they have been here above three months, in lodgings in Avon Street— a disgraceful place, but the cheapest they could find—and without even the means to return home again. And now they are so much in arrears in paying the rent, that they are threatened with eviction. Heaven knows when they last had a decent meal."

"But surely with the assistance you have provided him—"

"I could give him but a pittance. I hoped it might be enough to appease the landlady for at least a little while longer, and get them something to eat. But I fear it will not be enough. If only I had not—"

He stopped short, and was silent.

"If only you had not—?" she repeated.

He made her no answer, but only shook his head in response.

"I hope," said Anne in dismay, "you did not take upon yourself the expense of hiring my horse, Captain Turner, as well as the trouble."

He reddened as he replied, "I am afraid that act of gallantry was wholly out of my power."

When she looked doubtful, he added, "You will receive a bill from the ostler directly, Miss de Bourgh, I assure you."

"Then why—?"

He made her no answer, but looked exceedingly ill at ease as he leaned forward to fiddle with the arrangement of his bridle.

Recollecting again what Mr Wynnewood had told her of the captain's poverty, Anne began very much to fear that, between the hiring of his horse, and relieving Mr Gower's distress, he had spent all the ready money he possessed. She now felt persuaded he was too sensible a man to have been tempted into gaming; but though she could hardly suppose a captain of the Navy to be ill-paid, perhaps the better part of his income might go to supporting his widowed mother and sister. She knew so little of these matters! Heartily did she wish she could offer him her assistance, or at least urge him to confide his predicament to Mr Wynnewood. Whatever degree of impertinence the example of her mother might seem to authorise, however, Anne's own natural delicacy would not allow her to feel herself justified in questioning him further. She could only hope that, were her surmises correct, as a gentleman Captain Turner would have no difficulty in securing credit for his lodgings and other necessary expenses, until such time as his next cheque might be forwarded to him from the Admiralty.

Thus they rode on in silence a little while longer, each absorbed in private contemplation; until at last the sight of Mr and Miss Wynnewood riding towards them caused them both to dismiss the thoughts which had been occupying them, and to greet their overdue friends with every appearance of real pleasure.

Chapter 7

Great as Anne's enjoyment of the previous day's walk had been, today's ride bid fair to furnish still greater. The countryside through which they travelled—the stately hills with their wooded brows, the pastoral valleys with their tidy fields and open meadows, and, in their midst, the river Avon meandering with a tranquil grace—appeared to her so delightful that she could scarce imagine how much more lovely they would be a few months hence. The landscape alone would have been quite enough to ensure her gratification in the outing; but the added charm of Mr Wynnewood's companionship, and the attentions which had been growing more marked with every passing day, caused her to feel that life could accord her no greater happiness; and to believe it might not be many days more, before Mr Wynnewood would ask that question which would secure the continuance of her happiness forever.

So much at ease did she now feel with him, that when they entered into a wood, and the other two were for a time riding a little apart from them, she ventured to relate to him a part of her earlier conversation with Captain Turner, and to express her concern that the captain's generous impulse to help his old friend might have led him to exhaust his resources.

"What!" Mr Wynnewood burst out with a laugh. "Has poor Turner emptied his purse for some broken-down old sailor? Oh, he is a prize pigeon!"

Anne was taken aback. "But—was it not amiable in Captain Turner, to wish to come to his friend's aid?"

Mr Wynnewood, recollecting himself, said in a softer tone, "Of course—Turner is a good fellow. I said so before. But he ought to leave that sort of munificence to people of fortune, like you and me. We can afford it. He cannot."

"Then you do agree we ought to be charitable to the poor?"

"Indeed I do, Miss de Bourgh. Only the other day, for example, I gave a very considerable sum to the Mineral Water Hospital—but this must be kept just between ourselves," he added, "for of course I made the gift anonymously."

"Anonymously? Why did you make it anonymously?"

"Why, is not half the virtue in philanthropy lost, if one boasts about it? It would seem to be fishing for compliments, if one did not accomplish these things with as little fanfare as possible. Our rank in life demands that we must help those less fortunate than ourselves; why then should we make a great noise about doing what is no more than our duty?"

"I confess," said she, "I had never given it much thought before; but what you say does make a great deal of sense."

A moment later, they were again united with Louisa and Captain Turner, and soon after, they came to a narrow path through the wood where they were obliged to proceed in single file. This rendered conversation difficult; but as they rode on, Anne occupied her mind in reflecting on the subject of the conversation just ended. At Rosings Park, Lady Catherine was the dispenser of alms; Anne had never had aught to do with such matters. But though her mother was always liberal—judiciously liberal—to the poor, she certainly did not proffer her assistance quietly. On the contrary, she conferred charity with a kind of parading condescension, as her daughter had witnessed with a faint embarrassment on more than one occasion. Pondering Mr Wynnewood's remarks, the words 'Charity vaunteth not itself,' came unbidden into her mind; and she was compelled to acknowledge to herself the better philosophy of his practice, and to honour the warmth of heart which must lie beneath such thoughtful benevolence.

They rode on; and they were just emerging onto a broad, open expanse, when they were startled by the report of a gun in the wood close behind them. Anne gave a little cry of alarm and, before she could understand what had happened, found herself hurtling across the field at a fevered gallop, clinging to the mare's back with all the strength she possessed!

It was not George Wynnewood, however, who dashed off in pursuit of her, but Captain Turner. When the shot was fired, both the Wynnewoods' horses reared in fright, and Mr Wynnewood, after hastily reining in his own agitated animal, had then had all he could manage to try and steady his sister's. So Captain Turner, stopping only to see that Miss Wynnewood was being attended to by her brother, took it upon himself to go after Miss de Bourgh. He could not catch up to her very quickly, for she had a considerable running start of him; and it was not until her horse began of its own accord to slacken its pace, that he was able to pull up alongside her, and seize hold of the reins.

But great was his astonishment when at last he had succeeded in arresting her horse, and leapt down from his own to help her dismount; for he found her, not ready to faint with terror, as he had every reason to expect, but— radiant! Her eyes bright, her cheeks flushed—her whole countenance aglow with exhilaration!

"Miss de Bourgh!" he exclaimed, reaching up to assist her from the saddle. "You are not hurt?"

"No—not at all."

It was a foolish question to ask, he acknowledged to himself as she alighted, for the answer was plainly written on her face; but he was utterly perplexed. Though he had previously remarked with some interest the delight she seemed to take in even the simplest of pleasures, she had otherwise impressed him as rather a frail, faint-hearted sort of girl. How much entreaty it had taken, indeed, for her friends to persuade her to ride at all! Yet now —

"Were you not frightened when your horse bolted?" he asked.

"Oh! yes—I was terrified! I was sure I should be thrown, and killed—or at least very badly injured. One does hear of such things, after all. But it seemed better to try to hold on, than to jump off; so I just closed my eyes, and held on as tightly as I could. And then the strangest thing happened! After a little while I stopped thinking of the danger. I seemed to forget everything except—the feeling of the wind rushing past me—and the beating of the horse's hooves on the ground beneath me. And then I began to feel—as though I were flying! Oh, Captain, it was—it was quite the most thrilling feeling I have ever known!"

He laughed out loud in amazement—and she laughed too, in even greater amazement, perhaps, than he; and they stood, laughing and smiling, until with a sudden feeling of anxiety Anne remembered their companions.

"But what of Miss Wynnewood, and Mr Wynnewood?" she asked. "Are they all right?"

"Yes," he said. "That is, I believe so; but—"

At that very moment they heard a distant hallooing, and both turned to see Louisa and her brother coming toward them on foot, Mr Wynnewood leading their two horses by the reins. Anne and Captain Turner walked back with their own horses to meet them.

"Anne!" cried Miss Wynnewood as they approached. "Thank goodness you are unharmed; I thought surely we should all have our necks broken. That wretched man*, to fire off his gun so near us! I declare, I never was more frightened in my life!"

"My dear Miss de Bourgh," said Mr Wynnewood feelingly, taking up her hand in his, "I am very much relieved to see you safe. It was fortunate indeed that you had an open field to cross, and met with no obstruction! But are you quite certain you have suffered no injury?"

She assured him, with a blushing smile, that she was perfectly well; and he, still retaining her hand, gave her a smile in return which sent a flutter of happiness through her.

After a little deliberation, the four friends determined on resuming their ride, but resolved henceforth to keep only to the open areas, to avoid any further mishaps. Whilst this discussion took place, Mr Wynnewood continued to gaze upon Anne with an expression, as she believed, of ardent affection, and certainly one of real satisfaction in her safety. He relinquished her hand at length only to secure the felicity of assisting her back into the saddle. As they rode on again side by side, he talked of the very great anxiety he had felt at seeing her in danger, and of the agitation it had cost him to suffer Captain Turner to go after her when the shot was fired. Had it not been imperative for him to subdue his sister's horse at once, nothing, he assured her, could have prevented him from rescuing her himself.

That a man so perfect in every respect as Mr Wynne-wood was, would actually form an attachment to her—would single her out, as he had, almost from the first moment of their acquaintance—was a circumstance Anne could scarcely have imagined possible but a few weeks since; yet that Mr Wynnewood *was* attached seemed indisputable. Indeed, so nearly did he now approach to making his declaration in form that, had they been quite alone, Anne could hardly doubt she would have found herself a betrothed woman at the end of half an hour's time.

Some of my readers may be asking themselves, was there not any faint voice within, which whispered to Anne a little doubt as to the true merit of Mr Wynnewood's character? Was there not even the smallest suspicion in her mind, that perhaps his attachment had arisen too quickly, his courtship advanced too rapidly, to be altogether sincere? Had her novel-reading not taught her that a man may sometimes be something very different from what he appears?

Alas! it had not. She had read stories of such men, it is

true; but having lived so secluded a life, Anne de Bourgh was in fact remarkably naive for a woman well past the first blush of youth; and the circumstances under which she had become acquainted with the Wynnewoods—the fears and anxieties attendant upon her mother's accident, and the compassion and comfort the Wynnewoods had provided her in the face of that crisis, had been the means of promoting a sudden and singular sort of intimacy between them; and had given her a conviction of their goodness and integrity, which could not have been easily shaken.

Chapter 8

The remainder of the ride was as pleasurable as its beginning had been, and it concluded without further incident. Something of the glow Anne felt within her was a little dimmed, however, when she returned to Sydney Place to find Mr Collins, with all his eloquence in readiness, awaiting her.

"Miss de Bourgh!" he cried out as she walked past the door of the drawing room, where he had been fortifying himself with perusing a volume of sermons in anticipation of her arrival. Hoping to escape a private interview, she endeavoured to excuse herself to change out of her habit before engaging in any conversation. He would brook no evasion, however; and unluckily, there was no Mrs Collins at hand just then to deliver her. Therefore, though reluctantly, she allowed the reverend gentleman to conduct her to a seat, and submitted to the inevitable oration with at least a tolerable pretence of polite attention, divided between annoyance at his presumption and amusement at his absurdity.

"My dear Miss de Bourgh," he began, "I must beg leave humbly to apologise, if in addressing you thus, I am taking a liberty which seems not perfectly compatible with the deference I owe to you; but I shall not be prevented, even by a fear of appearing disrespectful to one for whom I must ever feel the highest degree of admiration and esteem, from fulfilling, to the very best of my ability, the responsibility entrusted to me by my noble patroness. Acting, as I am (whilst your honourable mother is unwell), somewhat in the character of guardian to you—"

Anne was momentarily roused to indignation. Mr Collins, her guardian! Good heavens—to what an abyss of indignity was she sunk! She was about to express her displeasure to him in such terms as even Lady Catherine's celebrated frankness could hardly have surpassed, when she thought of the clergyman's wife; and for that good lady's sake, she held her tongue. He continued,

"—I feel myself called upon to speak to you, principally in that capacity; but also as your religious preceptor, and indeed (may I be so bold to add?) as a concerned and sympathising friend. I have only lately discovered, from one of the servants who saw you depart this morning, the nature of your outing today with Mr Wynnewood and his sister; and holding all that family, as I assure you I do, in the highest respect, I do not now propose to dwell upon what I fear I must term a—a *transgression* of the rules of decorum, in an unmarried young lady's going out of the house without the attendance of a proper chaperon, and in company with only one other young lady, and two young gentlemen not related to her. On that matter, you may be assured that no further word shall pass my lips; I know I may safely leave it to your own excellent understanding, to lead you in time to a just appraisal of such conduct. But the significance of the aforementioned infraction pales, in comparison with the enormity of the second; and I must tell you, Miss de Bourgh, I could not be otherwise than profoundly troubled, when I learned that you had been persuaded recklessly to take part in that hazardous exercise, from which you have hitherto most prudently abstained. I must, therefore, take it upon myself to implore you: recollect the delicate fragility of your health—the devoted affection of your venerable mother—even the very continuance of the noble line of de Bourgh; of which, I feel it incumbent upon myself to remind you, you are the sole living representative, as well as the heiress of Rosings Park! Had the awful task fallen to me, of informing her ladyship that the eminent lineage of Sir Lewis de Bourgh was prematurely come to its final end — that her most beloved daughter's life was lost, and in a pursuit of no greater consequence than a pleasure-jaunt on horseback! — my dear Miss de Bourgh, devoted as I am to the interests of all your family, I hardly know how I should have brought myself to utter those fateful words! I am not inclined, I assure you, to shirk any of those sacred duties (no matter how disagreeable) which, as a matter of course, will devolve upon any gentleman who adopts the church as his chosen profession; but to destroy forever the happiness and tranquillity of that noble lady, is one task which, I fear, I could scarcely undertake to perform! No, such woeful tidings shall never be spoken by me, if there is aught I can do to prevent that tragedy from occurring. I do most humbly beseech you, therefore, to never again run so great a risk to your own safety, and to the peace of that most worthy of mothers — who even now is eagerly awaiting your return, and most anxious to speak with you."

"You have not told her — ?" Anne asked in some apprehension.

"Not as yet; and I promise you solemnly, that she shall never hear aught from me of this unfortunate affair, if you will but give me your word, my dear Miss de Bourgh, that henceforth you will eschew that particular form of recreation, the repeated practice of which must almost certainly end in calamity."

Again Anne felt the stirrings of rebellion within her breast. She had found her ride a thoroughly delightful experience, and one she most fervently wished to repeat. For once free of her mother's authority, was she now to submit to the dictates of such a one as Mr Collins? Indeed she would not!

And yet, after all, she did submit. Fear of her mother's displeasure was a great retarding weight. Solicitude for Captain Turner was another, albeit a lesser one. Persuaded as she was that the captain would not be able to afford the hire of his horse for another day, and not wishing him to be placed in an awkward position, should another ride be proposed—she ended by telling Mr Collins she would heed his advice, and would engage not to ride again, at least whilst she remained in Bath. With this pledge he was obliged to be satisfied; and with a deferential bow, and many compliments to her amiability and good sense, he at last suffered her to leave him. She hastened upstairs to change her clothes and, clad in a fresh gown, repaired to her mother's bedchamber without further delay.

Softly opening the door, she saw Lady Catherine lying in her bed, still much bandaged, with her eyes closed, and perhaps asleep. The nurse, Mrs Fitch, a tidy, heavyset woman, sat knitting in a chair by the fire. Anne lingered a moment in the doorway, uncertain whether to advance or retreat, when her ladyship's eyes opened and she perceived her daughter hesitating at the threshold.

"Come here, Anne," she said. "I wish—to speak to you. Fitch—leave us alone," she ordered the nurse, who promptly put aside her needles, rose and departed.

Anne could not but smile a little. However feeble in body, Lady Catherine was yet Lady Catherine; and however halting might be her speech, she could not speak but to command.

Anne seated herself in a chair by her mother's bedside, and asked her how she was.

"I am no better," said her ladyship, soliciting no sympathy, "but there is another matter—of particular importance, Anne—which I wish to discuss with you. Mrs Wynnewood has again been sitting with me today."

"I hope you had a pleasant visit with her, ma'am?"

Lady Catherine did not answer at once. Her eyes closed for a few moments, then opened again.

"You will hardly be surprised at—what I have to tell you. Mrs Wynnewood confided to me that her son—that Mr George Wynnewood—is quite taken with you—and means shortly to make you —an offer of marriage."

Anne blushed, and looked away in some confusion.

Though she had, in the privacy of her thoughts, been dreaming of just such an eventuality, to hear from her mother's lips that all she had been imagining was about to be accomplished in reality, put her into a little flurry of agitation. She was happy, of course, very happy, to have all her dearest hopes confirmed; yet she felt strangely unsettled, too. But she readily concluded it was Lady Catherine's manner of questioning her—the speaking so bluntly on so delicate a subject, which rendered her ill at ease.

"Has he done so, Anne?" her ladyship queried. "Has Mr Wynnewood made you an offer of marriage?"

"No, ma'am," Anne replied after a little hesitation. "Not as yet."

"But you do expect it?"

"I—I do not know. I think perhaps he might," she admitted.

"He shall, most certainly. Tomorrow—or the day after, at the latest. Now tell me at once—what answer do you intend to give him?"

"If Mr Wynnewood should make me an offer, I—I believe I would accept him. That is," she amended hastily, "if you approve, ma'am."

"I do," said Lady Catherine. "This is precisely the sort of match, Anne—which I have long been wishing for you. A gentleman of very large fortune—of extensive property—of excellent family on both sides. He has not a title, as I should have preferred. But he is very good-looking, which—though hardly of so much consequence as his other qualifications—is not to be dismissed as insignificant, either."

Her eyes closed again. "I have always intended my grandchildren should be handsome," she added weakly. After another little interval, she opened her eyes once more.

"The matter is settled, then. You have done very well, Anne. I congratulate you."

Her eyelids drooped yet again. She appeared quite depleted by the exertion of speaking so much.

"I will rest now, Anne—you may go," said her ladyship, her eyes remaining closed. "Send Fitch back in to me when you leave."

Anne felt a sudden, inexplicable impulse to kiss the prostrate woman who had so long held dominion over her; but she did not act on it. Her relationship with Lady Catherine had never had much of warmth in it, and most likely her mother would only have been irritated by such a sentimental gesture.

After she had withdrawn from the room, and dispatched a servant to fetch Mrs Fitch back from the kitchen, Anne stood musing for some time in the corridor, thinking of her mother, and of Mr Wynnewood, and of everything that had happened since their coming to Bath. At length, however, she was awakened from her reverie by the sound of voices downstairs. One of them belonged to Mr Collins, and the other to Mr Nichols, the surgeon, who was come to see Lady Catherine as he did every afternoon at about this time. Having something particular which she wished to discuss with him, but desiring to avoid another encounter with the clergyman, she waited at the top of the stairs for the surgeon to ascend. He did so at last (for he, too, found it no easy task to detach himself from Mr Collins), greeting her as he reached the top, and expressing a hope that her ladyship was a little better today.

She told him she believed his patient was about the same. Then she asked, would he do her the kindness of speaking with her for a few minutes on another matter? He complied with ready civility; and, after glancing about to be sure they would not be overheard, she commenced upon a resolution formed earlier that day.

Briefly, she described to him the situation of Captain Turner's unfortunate friends, the Gowers. She knew Mr Nichols to be connected professionally with the hospital; could he possibly use his influence to have Mrs Gower admitted for treatment?

"I am very sorry to disappoint you, Miss de Bourgh," said he, "but indeed I cannot. I am afraid the hospital rules are very strict as to this point: no patient may be admitted without the requisite letters from his own parish, and the prior approval of the doctors. Moreover, there is a waiting list for admission, and no one may be admitted out of turn."

"But surely exceptions must be made from time to time?" she persisted. "If the rules might be set aside in this one case, I would be more than happy to make a donation—a substantial donation to the hospital. I am very anxious to help the family in question, you see—and I can assure you of their being very deserving."

"Again, I am sorry," he repeated. "The hospital depends upon the generous donations of its many benefactors; and we would certainly be exceedingly grateful to you, ma'am, should you choose to make a contribution towards its continued operation. But the rules cannot be circumvented."

"However," said Anne after a few moments' reflection, "there is no reason I could not arrange for Mrs Gower to be treated privately for her condition, is there?"

"None whatever."

"And would you be willing, Mr Nichols, to visit Mrs Gower yourself? You would greatly oblige me—"

"I am afraid, ma'am, that between my work at the hospital, and my private practice, I have not the time to undertake it. But I can recommend to you another surgeon, a Mr Hubbard—rather a young man, and only lately established in Bath, but very competent. I believe he would be quite willing to take the case. I expect to see him after I leave here today, and I should be happy to arrange it for you, if you wish."

She expressed her gratitude to him most warmly, and authorised him to offer the commission to the young surgeon. She desired him to ask if Mr Hubbard would further oblige her by settling with the Gowers' landlady, on her behalf, for the payment of arrears in their rent, and arranging as well for board to be provided to them, also at her expense; and she stipulated most emphatically that everything was to be done without mention of her own name. She was to be referred to only as 'an anonymous benefactor'.

Unfortunately, she explained, she did not know the Gowers' precise address; but she assumed Mr Hubbard would have little difficulty in locating them with the information she could supply: he need only enquire in Avon Street, for a man named Gower, with a wooden leg, and a sickly wife.

Chapter 9

Overnight the weather turned windy and colder, and by the time Anne awoke in the morning, a thick, blowing rain had set in. Gazing from her window at the gloomy sky above and the wet street below, she hoped the rain would not deter her friends from calling on her that day. Surely even Louisa and her brother would not be so intrepid as to walk to Sydney Place, as was their custom, in such a downpour; but she trusted they could not object to taking out their carriage on this occasion, however they might dislike making use of it in general.

At about half past eleven, however, she received the following note from Louisa:

My dearest Anne,

Rain is an odious invention—at present I can recollect no purpose it has ever served, save to enrich the makers of pattens and umbrellas! I fear this abominable weather must prevent me from having the happiness of calling on you this morning. Lest you should be inclined to tax me with willful neglect, my dearest friend, I must tell you that my brother and I were dressed and ready to come to you, when our coachman informed us there was something amiss with one of the carriage wheels, and it was not safe to be taken out. You may imagine our wretchedness. My poor brother is quite wild with vexation, and I am very much afraid he may end by walking to Sydney Place in the rain (as he vows he will) unless my mother and I can dissuade him.

I have often observed, however, that the most violent storms often clear away most quickly; so I shall venture to hope this one will do the same. If it does, be assured that we will come to you as soon as may be. Until then I remain

Most aff'ly yours,
Louisa Wynnewood

Anne sat in her room debating for some time, after reading this note, whether she ought to send her own carriage to the South Parade, to convey Louisa and her brother to Sydney Place. She would not have hesitated a moment to do so, but that the conversation with her mother the day before had strangely discomposed her, making her feel suddenly shy and unsure of herself. In truth, she had until then been experiencing Mr Wynnewood's courtship almost as if it were a story in a novel; but Lady Catherine's stamp of approval made it all seem so much more real—and somewhat unsettling. Of George Wynnewood's worthiness she could feel no mistrust: he was perfection itself. Was it possible, then, she had rather not be married at all?

Scarcely had she begun sorting through this perplexity of emotion, when one of the maids came to tell her that a gentleman awaited her downstairs. Her pulses were at once all alive with the certainty that it was Mr Wynnewood, come on foot in the midst of a deluge because the ardour of his attachment would allow him to delay his proposal no longer! Could she meet such passionate affection with doubt or irresolution? Impossible! She steadied herself as best she could, and went down to give her acceptance.

She might have spared herself a good deal of agitation, however, had she thought first to make enquiry as to the name of her caller; for as she came down the stairs, she beheld Charlotte Collins standing near the landing, conversing, not with George Wynnewood, but with Captain Turner. Upon seeing her, that gentleman eagerly came forward and began to address her; while Mrs Collins quietly excused herself and retreated to join Mrs Jenkinson in the sitting room hard by, leaving the doors ajar.

So great was Anne's confusion and discomfiture at her own mistake, that she could not at first meet the captain's eye, nor attend to what he was saying. At length, however, she began to comprehend that he was speaking of the Gowers; and she endeavoured to collect herself, and to listen with better attention.

"Imagine my astonishment, Miss de Bourgh," said he, "when I went to call on my friends this morning in Avon Street, and heard from them that a surgeon had been there already that morning—sent to administer to Mrs Gower by a person who, as they were told, wished not to be named—and who, moreover, had seen to it that the bill for their rent was settled, and victuals ordered to be provided to them! They were perfectly convinced it had all been done by me; and I was at the greatest pains to persuade them otherwise!"

There was an animation in his manner just then, an earnestness in his gaze, which rendered Anne still more confused and self-conscious than she had been before. It was therefore not till a few moments afterward that she first perceived he was very wet. Apparently, he had equipped himself with neither umbrella nor hat to shield him from the weather: his hair was plastered down all about his head by the rain, and his coat was dripping.

"Good heavens, Captain," she exclaimed, "you are soaked through! Do come into the parlour and warm yourself by the fire."

"It is quite unnecessary—I shall not impose upon you, ma'am. But you must allow me to thank you for your extraordinary kindness to my old friend. I assure you, I did not yesterday make known to you the Gowers' misfortunes, in the hope or expectation of your doing anything for them. Indeed I should never have mentioned them to you at all, had you not pursued the subject. I certainly had not the smallest idea you would take such a charge upon yourself; and I hardly know how to express warmly enough the gratitude I feel, for all you have done for them."

"But," said Anne with some chagrin, "why should you think it was I who helped your friends? If the assistance was given anonymously—as you said it was—it might have been anyone."

"Because there is no one else who knows of their distress, who is at the same time possessed of the means to relieve it. It cannot have been anyone but yourself."

"What about Mr Wynnewood? Did it not occur to you that he, perhaps—?"

He shook his head. "No. I know it was none of his doing—. But I must beg your pardon, Miss de Bourgh. You desired your identity to be kept secret; and from your unwillingness to own the deed to me now, it is plain you wish it to remain so. I have allowed the warmth of my feelings to get the better of my discretion, and repaid your generosity most unhandsomely. I will press you no further. I will only say, good day to you, ma'am, and—God bless you!" With these words, he took up her hand and raised it for a moment to his lips, before he turned to go. He had just entered the vestibule when she called out his name, and hurried after him.

"Please," she said as they stood together in the entryway, "at least allow me to send you home in the carriage. You ought not to be out walking in such dreadful weather."

"No, no, there is no need to trouble your coachman. I do not mind the rain at all. I am an old seafarer, you know," he said with a smile. "I have been out in many a worse storm than this."

"But I was intending to send the carriage out anyway, to bring Miss Wynnewood here; and you might oblige me by delivering my message to her—if you would be so good."

"I will be more than happy," he said with a bow, "to do anything you ask, Miss de Bourgh. But I wonder that you should think it necessary to send your carriage for Miss Wynnewood; has not she a carriage of her own to take her wherever she wishes to go?"

"Yes, of course," she answered. "But she and Mr Wynnewood had been just about to come here, when they discovered one of the wheels of their carriage was broken; and she sent me word that, on that account, they could not come. So I thought I might as well send my carriage to the South Parade, to bring them here. And indeed, Captain, if you have no other engagement—I should be very glad if you would join us. I am sure, even with our small party, we will have a very cheerful day together, in spite of the weather."

The little frown which had formed on the captain's brow as she explained about the Wynnewoods' broken carriage wheel, now cleared off, and was replaced by another smile. He would be delighted to accept her invitation, he told her; and Anne settled it for him that he would first take her carriage back to his own lodgings in Westgate Buildings, to change into dry clothing, and would then drive over to the South Parade for Miss Wynnewood and her brother, and bring them back to Sydney Place. With difficulty, she also persuaded him to wait in the parlour by the fire until the carriage was ready, though he could not be prevailed upon to spoil any of her chairs by sitting on them.

While he waited with Anne, Mrs Collins, and Mrs Jenkinson, he talked; expressing himself, as a gentleman of education and experience commonly will do, very pleasantly. In response to Anne's questions, he spoke of his last ship, the *Amphitrite*: she was a 16-gun sloop, and he had had the command of her for nearly five years. He was made Captain in consequence of that action in which he had been wounded more than a year ago, but was presently waiting to be posted into another ship. He hoped he should have the good fortune to get a frigate; but while the current peace held, he should count himself lucky indeed to get anything at all.

After he had gone, Mrs Jenkinson remarked that he seemed a most agreeable young man.

"Yes," said Anne. "But I do feel rather sorry for him. He is in love with Miss Wynnewood, you know."

"Is he, indeed?" said Mrs Collins.

"Oh! yes," Anne replied. "Though I am afraid the poor Captain has not much chance of winning her affections. Louisa is so very beautiful! Is not she?"

"Yes, very beautiful."

"And Captain Turner is not a handsome man," said Mrs Jenkinson.

"No. Not handsome," Anne acquiesced hesitatingly. "Not quite handsome; but still, there is something rather pleasing in his countenance, I think. Would not you agree, Mrs Collins?"

"Indeed. But as to his being an admirer of Miss Wynnewood's—I think I should have said the captain rather admired *you*, Miss de Bourgh."

"Me! Good heavens, Mrs Collins, what can have given you such a notion? You are quite mistaken."

"I daresay I am. It was only a certain warmth in his manner toward you; but if, as you say, he is in love with Miss Wynnewood, I must have misconstrued his looks. He was grateful to you for helping his friends; no doubt the expression I observed was merely the effect of gratitude."

Anne agreed. It was gratitude only—it could have been nothing else.

Chapter 10

Charlotte Collins, when she was still Miss Lucas, once wisely said that there are very few of us who have heart enough to be really in love without encouragement; and it must be owned that Captain Turner, though courageous in battle, was no braver in love than most.

When he was introduced to Miss Louisa Wynnewood, he thought her the most beautiful creature he had ever beheld. But the long walk in Sydney Gardens had been enough to persuade him that, though beautiful, elegant, and well-bred, she was not precisely the woman to suit him. How readily he might have begun to perceive her imperfections, had she shown any decided preference for his society, may be conjectured; but wanting that encouragement, he quickly detected in her a lack of warmth and openness, which saved him from regretting the impossibility of attaching her.

But (as Mrs Collins herself had so astutely observed) he was now beginning instead to feel some interest in Miss de Bourgh. He had not, it is true, thought her pretty when they first met; but he had since discovered her to be possessed of an ingenuousness and a goodness of heart which illumined her countenance, and gave her, in his eyes, a beauty she could not otherwise have claimed. While so many ladies of her age and station appeared to him strangely wearied of life, Miss de Bourgh seemed to find the greatest pleasure in every experience—almost as if the world itself were new to her. Her wonderful delight at being run away with by her horse (a circumstance which would have reduced most women to a state of hysteria) had charmed him, and caused him to look on her with a fresh attention.

Then, in this susceptible condition, he learned of the quick and careful assistance she had rendered his poor friends. He was not unaccustomed to witness such liberality among the brotherhood of the Navy; but to meet with it in society *generally,* was not what he had ever before had cause to expect. No doubt she was rich, and could afford to be charitable; but many with wealth equal even to Miss de Bourgh's, would not have troubled themselves in the least to come to the aid of persons so wholly unknown to them.

Captain Turner acknowledged to himself a strong inclination to see more of her. Nonetheless, it was likely to prove no more fortunate an inclination than a preference for Miss Wynnewood would have been; for Miss de Bourgh's partiality for George Wynnewood was all too apparent— and apparently reciprocated. As he was by no means in love with her as yet, however, the captain might from his heart have wished them both happy. Unfortunately, he had begun to feel a little uneasiness as regarded the present character of his former friend, which gave him some alarm on Miss de Bourgh's account, should their mutual attachment lead to marriage.

Despite all appearances to the contrary, Captain Turner had arrived in Bath well-supplied with ready money. He was not wealthy; he was at present on half pay, and, as Anne herself had guessed, the better part of his income was apportioned to the maintenance of his mother and sister. Nonetheless, he had brought with him more than enough to meet the modest needs of a single gentleman not given to expensive habits, for a residence of some duration.

On the very first day of his reunion with George Wynnewood in Bond Street, however, that gentleman had asked him for a loan of one hundred pounds. He had assured the captain he would be able to pay him back in full almost immediately—most certainly before the end of another week. That a young man possessed of a great fortune should be occasionally short of cash, was too common a story to awaken Captain Turner's distrust. The sum of one hundred pounds, besides, was far too small to be of any use to George Wynnewood, if he were in any serious financial difficulty. Never one to refuse the reasonable request of a friend, he complied without hesitation, though it had taken most of what he had on hand to do so. It was for this reason that, after paying for the hire of his horse the following morning, he had not money enough left to assist his other old friend, Gower.

He began to entertain some doubts, however, when they all met to go riding. Knowing, as he did, a great deal about horses, he readily perceived that the mounts ridden by both Wynnewood and his sister were none of the best; he suspected them to be hired, like his own and Miss de Bourgh's, only hired more cheaply. He also observed that Miss Wynnewood's habit was rather a shabby one for a young lady of wealth and fashion to be attired in; and that Wynnewood's own boots were a good deal too scuffed and disreputable for any tolerably self-respecting valet to have had a hand in the care of them.

Later that day, he asked Wynnewood if he could let him have back a few pounds, out of the hundred he had given him the day before. Wynnewood was very sorry — hated to disappoint him — had he only known, &c. — but the money was already gone. He had that morning paid off his landlord, as well as the butcher, the chandler, and sundry other tradesmen with whom his family had run up an assortment of little bills during their stay at Bath. His mother, he said, was very keen on keeping all their accounts current; and so, to preserve her from any feeling of unhappiness on that score, he had discharged them promptly.

The Captain could not but question the truth of this story. The family had been in Bath only a short while, and could hardly have run up bills enough to be a matter of anxiety for a lady in Mrs Wynnewood's presumably easy circumstances; such people commonly thought nothing of leaving tradesmen's bills owing for many months. It seemed equally unlikely George Wynnewood would have been so conscientious in discharging these small debts as to leave not even five pounds of pocket money for his own use. The explanation of the broken carriage wheel, too, was highly dubious, and seemed to Captain Turner a further proof that Wynnewood's position was not what he professed it to be.

Where, then, had the hundred pounds gone? The Captain very much feared it had gone at the gaming table. To his knowledge, George Wynnewood had inherited a large estate and a magnificent fortune from his father. To live beyond an income such as he must have enjoyed was no mean feat, and could scarcely have been accomplished save by the most reckless kind of speculation, or at high stakes play—perhaps both. Captain Turner did not believe his old friend to be unusually greedy by nature, nor at all lacking in understanding; but alas, it required neither an uncommon degree of avarice, nor of imbecility, to succumb to the temptations of the gaming house, or the promise of easy gain.

His suspicions, if true, boded very ill for Miss de Bourgh, the captain reflected as he arrived at Westgate Buildings and repaired to his rooms to change out of his wet clothing. He would not think so unkindly of George Wynnewood as to imagine he courted Miss de Bourgh only to secure her fortune. If he himself found the lady appealing, there was no reason to suppose his friend might not find her equally so. But if Wynnewood was indeed capable of exhausting, by whatever means, an inheritance of perhaps two hundred thousand pounds in just ten years, there could be little doubt he would speedily bring his wife to ruin as well, if given the power to do so.

It was an exceedingly delicate matter, and he knew not how to proceed. He wished to protect Miss de Bourgh if he could; but he could hardly denounce his friend to her, on the basis solely of suspicion and conjecture. If her mother were approachable, perhaps he might find some way of putting her on her guard without making any decided accusations. He knew nothing of Lady Catherine, but Mrs Jenkinson had mentioned her as a very prudent and sagacious woman. Incapacitated as she was at present, however, she could not be relied upon to ensure her daughter's safety. Mrs Jenkinson herself was far too meek, he felt, to be of use in such a matter as this; and Mr Collins he readily dismissed as incapable of acting with anything like tact or judgment.

But what of *Mrs* Collins? If her husband was wholly lacking in sense and discretion, she appeared to possess both qualities in good measure. Speaking with her earlier, he had marked her quiet intelligence. Might he drop a little hint to her about his apprehensions? Mrs Collins had known Miss de Bourgh much longer than he had, and together they could determine how best to act. If it became necessary, he concluded as he climbed back into Miss de Bourgh's carriage, this seemed the most appropriate course.

Still, he could not see his way clear to taking such a step at this juncture; he could only resolve on observing the Wynnewoods more narrowly for the time being. He had at present no real evidence to justify his suspicions; and it would be unjust and disloyal to expose his friend to the suspicions of others, without better proof than he now possessed.

Unbeknownst to him, however, Mrs Collins had already taken the precaution of initiating an enquiry into Mr Wynnewood's circumstances. Miss de Bourgh's fortune and property, as well as her future happiness, would be entrusted to the man she chose to marry; and Charlotte — though without any particular reason, beyond the rapidity of his courtship, to suspect Mr Wynnewood — deemed it wise to be guarded, where so much was at stake.

Not far from where her parents, Sir William and Lady Lucas, resided, lived a family by the name of Goulding; Mrs Goulding and Lady Lucas were old and intimate friends. Mr Goulding, a most respectable gentleman, was a native of Hertfordshire, but his wife had been born and bred in Cumberland—indeed, in that very part of Cumberland from which the Wynnewoods hailed; and though it was many years since she had made her home there, she still had numerous connections in that country. Mrs Collins, therefore, when writing to her mother to ask after the health of her little boy, had also asked her to call on Mrs Goulding at Haye-Park, to ascertain whether that lady had any knowledge of the Wynnewood family; and requested her to report back speedily any intelligence thus obtained. She was consequently in hopes of soon having the power to acquaint Lady Catherine and Miss de Bourgh with all the particulars of Mr Wynnewood's fortune, and of his character.

Chapter 11

Anne welcomed her friends to Sydney Place later that day with a little residue of the shyness she had been feeling since the previous evening; but Louisa's cheerful friendliness soon put her at her ease again, and Mr Wynnewood's attentive looks at once revived, undiminished, all those tender sentiments she had been cherishing from their first meeting at the Pump Room.

"Dear Anne," cried Louisa as she entered the drawing room and embraced her friend, "How good of you to send the captain for us with your carriage! It was the very thing I had been wishing for when I wrote you, but could not think it right to ask. In our enforced captivity my brother and I had been making ourselves so very disagreeable, that I daresay my mother was quite delighted to be rid of us at last."

"Indeed, Miss de Bourgh," said Mr Wynnewood, "your kindness has rescued us from a most horrible fate! Louisa and I should have been at daggers drawn, had we been obliged to endure another half-hour at home with only each other for company."

He offered a very courteous greeting to Mrs Jenkinson, stationed in a chair by the fire with her needlework; and another to Mrs Collins, situated at a desk in one corner of the room, where she was occupied in examining the household accounts. These civilities were echoed by Miss Wynnewood and the captain, and returned by the two women. Mr Wynnewood then settled himself beside Anne on one sofa, and his sister and Captain Turner seated themselves on the other.

"How very dreary this weather is!" Miss Wynnewood exclaimed after a little silence. "And how stupid you are today, George. Cannot you think of anything to amuse us with?"

"I had always thought," said her brother, "it was the province of *ladies* to keep the *gentlemen* entertained."

"Beastly creature! I should have expected more gallantry from you."

"Very well, Louisa," said he after a moment's pause. "I shall be as gallant as you please, and propose that we should at once form a little dancing party among ourselves. Will that provide you sufficient amusement? It would need but a minute to push back the furniture, and to take up the rug; and if Mrs Jenkinson would be so good as to submit to play for us—for I cannot doubt, ma'am," (to that lady) "that you play exceedingly well, and are a great proficient in country-dances and concertos alike—why, though we are but two couple to stand up, I for one will find nothing to complain of in such an arrangement; that is, if Miss de Bourgh will consent to honour me with her hand."

"I should be most happy to oblige you at the pianoforte, sir," said Mrs Jenkinson before Anne could reply, "but Miss de Bourgh does not dance."

"I suppose," said Mr Wynnewood dryly, "that her health prevents her."

"Indeed, it does, sir. She is, unhappily, too delicate for such an exertion, and has never undertaken it."

He turned to Anne with a satirical eye. "What say you, Miss de Bourgh? Is it true—you do not dance?"

"I—I am afraid I do not."

"Indeed. Nor do you ride, as you informed us the other day."

"But, Mr Wynnewood—" said Anne.

"Owing to your delicate health," said he, "you have no accomplishments whatever. You do not draw; you are too weak to move your pencil over a drawing pad. You do not sing; you could not muster breath enough to deliver a note."

"My dear sir," said Mrs Jenkinson, "I do protest—"

"You do not play, of course," he went on. "You might sit at the piano, perhaps, but could never find strength enough to strike the keys."

"Mr Wynnewood, do be serious!" said Anne, laughing.

"You speak no languages, and are ignorant of all literature and history, and all philosophy, both ancient and modern; you are far too frail to open a book, let alone read one."

His lips curved into an irresistible smile. "Now, you must not persist in this make-believe any longer, Miss de Bourgh. You are no more sickly than I am myself. We have all seen how well you ride, and I have not the smallest doubt we shall find you equally skilled at dancing."

"Indeed," she admitted, "I do not mean to say that I *could not* dance—that is, I do not *know* that I could not—but I have never learned how."

"Never learned to dance!" he exclaimed. "Can it be so?"

She assured him that it was.

"Well then," said he, "I can only say that your education has been most shamefully neglected. I say so even before good Mrs Jenkinson there, who had the superintending of it. Nay, were Lady Catherine herself present, I should not scruple to declare it to her as well, as she perhaps bears the greatest responsibility for having allowed so shocking a deficiency to continue as long as it has."

"Really, sir," began Mrs Jenkinson, "I do not think—"

"I beg your pardon, ma'am. I know you are too kind to take offense at my levity. And in fact, it is of no use to concern ourselves with who is or is not to blame for this woeful situation. We should rather seek at once to remedy it."

With this he stood up, and, taking matters into his own hands, gave his prescription, and saw that it was followed. Servants were called in to clear a space for them, and Mrs Jenkinson was perforce seated before the pianoforte. Most fortuitously, Mr Collins entered the room just then, having left her ladyship asleep, and he and his wife were pressed, in such a way as left them no power of refusal, to join the dance. Mrs Collins relinquished her accounts, and Mr Collins, with an ingratiating speech of only moderate length, led her forward to join the other two couples on the floor. In a most charming and attentive manner, Mr Wynne-wood then instructed Anne as to the figures they were to perform for the first dance, and when she had got them in her head reasonably well, gave Mrs Jenkinson the signal to begin playing.

It was an activity productive of much merriment. Mr Wynnewood and his sister were excellent dancers, their movements fluid, graceful, and elegant. They both laughed heartily at Anne's many missteps, but with so much good will, and such an appearance of partiality and affection for her, as only added to her delight. Captain Turner, who had been previously rather grave and silent, was soon smiling too. He danced rather well, Anne thought, but not so well as Mr Wynnewood. Even the Collinses seemed to be enjoying themselves. Mr Collins was an awkward, heavy-footed dancer, and committed nearly as many blunders as Anne did; but the clumsiness of his performance, though it caused him to be constantly apologising, seemed not to interfere at all with his gratification in the dance, nor even much with his wife's. Once again, Anne could not but wonder a little at the latter's composure in the face of her husband's oddities. She could only suppose that, as Mrs Collins had few opportunities of dancing, perhaps the pleasure she found in the diversion exceeded the pain occasioned by Mr Collins' conduct, which must have been endured no matter what the pursuit.

By the end of an hour's practice, Mr Wynnewood pronounced Anne so adept as to be quite ready to make her debut at either the Upper Rooms or the Lower whenever she chose, and expressed a hope that she would accompany

Louisa and himself thither one evening next week. Anne accepted his invitation, her eyes aglow with pleasure. This settled, they were all willing to submit to Mrs Jenkinson's entreaties that they would stop, before Miss de Bourgh should become over-fatigued; and Anne, unused to so much exercise, did own herself a little tired. Mr Collins, having till then quite forgotten Miss de Bourgh's invalid state, and feeling at once his remissness not only in having permitted the dancing to proceed, but in having implicitly given it his sanction by taking part, added his own pleas to Mrs Jenkinson's; and, as they all returned to their seats, could not satisfy himself without offering a long sermon in which were blended a curious mixture of obeisance, admonition, and apology.

The others politely allowed him to go on for some time, until Mr Wynnewood seized upon a brief pause to interject,

"Now, Miss de Bourgh, what shall we attempt for the next phase of your education? Do you draw?"

"No."

"Sing?"

"No."

"Play?"

"No—not a note."

He narrowed his eyes, deliberating for a few moments.

"Drawing and playing would take considerable instruction. But it would be nothing teach you to sing a little—if you are inclined to learn?"

"Oh! yes. I should like to learn, very much."

"Your speaking voice has quite a pleasing tone," he continued, with yet another of his irresistible smiles, "which promises well for singing. If Louisa will give me her assistance—"

"Of course," said Louisa obligingly.

"—I cannot doubt we shall have you warbling like the proverbial songbird, before the evening is over."

He asked whether there were any song she could remember to have heard at least a few times—one with a simple tune would be best. At first she could not recollect any song in particular; and they were all more than a bit surprised when Mrs Jenkinson, after a little hesitation, timidly suggested,

"I think you must remember *The Lady of Carlisle*, Miss de Bourgh, do you not? It was a favourite of your dear father's, you know. 'Down in Carlisle there lived a lady—'"

"Yes!" cried Anne. "'A lady beautiful and gay—'"

"Do you know it, Louisa?" asked Mr Wynnewood. In answer, Miss Wynnewood walked over to the pianoforte and, after seating herself, began to play, and to sing in a clear, pretty voice,

"Down in Carlisle, there lived a lady,
Being most beautiful and gay,
She vowed forever to stay a maiden;
No man should win her heart away,

"Unless it was a man of honour,
A man of honour, and high degree.
Then approached two noble brothers
This fair lady for to see,

"The first one being a brave lieutenant,
A brave lieutenant, a man of war;
The other being a bold sea captain
Late returned from a distant shore.

"Up then spoke this fair young lady:
'I can be but one man's bride.
If you both will ride with me,
Betwixt you twain I shall decide.'

"She ordered her a span of horses,
A span of horses at her command,
And onward then these three did ride
Until they came to the lions' den.

"There she stopped and there she halted;
She threw her fan in the lions' den,
Saying 'Which of you to gain a lady
Will return her fan again?'

"Up then spoke the brave lieutenant
In a voice both firm and low,
'I am a dear lover of women —
But I will not give my life for you.'

"Up then spoke the brave sea captain,
With a hearty voice he gave a cry,
'I am a dear lover of women —
I will return your fan or die!'

"The lions' den he boldy entered,
The lions fierce and wild within;
But he walked around and in among them
And safely returned her fan again.

"When she saw her true love coming,
Seeing no harm to him was done,
She threw herself against his breast,
Saying, 'Here is the prize that you have won!'
Saying, 'Here is the prize that you have won!'"

When the song was concluded, Miss Wynnewood's audience bestowed on her a profusion of compliments. Anne was much impressed by her friend's ability.

"If I had so beautiful a voice as you have, Louisa," said she, "I am sure I should always be singing. Indeed, when I think of all your accomplishments, and my own want of any, I feel quite ashamed of myself."

"But Miss de Bourgh," said Mrs Jenkinson, "You know your fragile state of health has always prevented—"

"No, ma'am!" Anne cried. "Dear Mrs Jenkinson, I pray you will forgive me, but Mr Wynnewood is right! That is—I will not say that I was *always* quite so well as I am now—and I know that you and my mother have had only my interest at heart. I suppose I truly was in indifferent health, at one time. But whatever infirmity I may have suffered in the past, clearly it exists no longer. And I cannot—I will not be prevented from doing what I choose, hereafter. And what is more, I mean to stop taking Mr Holt's Elixir—for it is a nauseating brew, and I am persuaded it has never done me any good!"

At this outburst, Mrs Jenkinson looked perfectly astonished, and a little frightened. Anne felt a little frightened herself at her own boldness! Mr Collins seemed not to know how to react, and was for once speechless. The rest of her companions, however, were smiling their approbation, and from Mrs Collins, there was a barely audible 'bravo'. Mr Wynnewood and his sister gave forth a little effusion of applause, and Anne felt almost giddy with excitement as Mr Wynnewood rose, holding out his hand to her, and led her to the pianoforte for her first singing lesson.

Mr Collins now recollected a commission he had promised to fulfill for her ladyship, and excused himself; while Mrs Collins returned to her accounts, and Mrs Jenkinson to her needlework. The lesson proceeded very well, however, without their assistance; and gave sufficient proof that, if not quite a *virtuosa*, Miss Anne de Bourgh was an apt pupil, had a tolerably pleasing voice, and was not lacking in taste.

However, when her throat after a time grew a little hoarse, she found it necessary to leave off singing. Miss Wynnewood then entreated Captain Turner to accompany her in a duet; and Mr Wynnewood, upon their beginning to sing together, led Anne away from the pianoforte and over to the window. There, with the noise of the piano to ensure his words would not be heard by any ears but hers, he declared, in the warmest terms, his passionate attachment to herself; and begged she would give him the immeasurable happiness of becoming his wife.

Chapter 12

Any misgivings Anne might have been feeling concerning the matrimonial state vanished in the face of Mr Wynnewood's tender ardour. His proposal was most joyfully accepted, and the happy gentleman pressed her to name an early day for that ceremony to be performed which would elevate him to still greater felicity. For his own satisfaction, next week—nay, *tomorrow* would not be too soon; and he hoped she would have pity on his cheerless solitary state, and put an end to it as quickly as possible.

Here a little difficulty arose. Though she knew her mother approved the match, Anne could not think it right that the wedding should take place until Lady Catherine was recovered from her injuries. Mr Wynnewood, however, thought her ladyship too affectionate a mother to wish the marriage delayed on her account. After a little discussion, they determined on Mr Wynnewood's sending his own mother to call at Sydney Place the following morning, to discuss the wedding plans with Lady Catherine, and allowing the two ladies to decide the question between them. Mr Wynnewood was confident they would rule in his favour.

They also determined to make no announcement to their friends, until both Lady Catherine and Mrs Wynnewood had been apprised of their engagement, and given it their formal sanction; but from the gentleman's high gaiety of manner, and the luminous expression of the lady's countenance, Mrs Collins deduced—Captain Turner feared—Miss Wynnewood knew what had occurred.

Mr Wynnewood, indeed, had earlier confided to his

sister that he meant to declare himself that day, if opportunity offered; and Louisa had taken it upon herself to provide the opportunity, by asking the captain to sing with her. Thus, she could not but assume George had seized upon it, to make his application to Miss de Bourgh; and his brilliant smile, when they were all assembled around the piano again, told her he had not asked in vain.

Captain Turner's eyes, even whilst he was singing with Miss Wynnewood, had been often turned towards that division of the room where Miss de Bourgh stood at the window, talking in low tones with Mr Wynnewood. He doubted not that Wynnewood was at that very moment soliciting her hand. Knowing she must surely consent to give it, the captain's uneasiness rose almost to alarm. He felt the keenest interest in Miss de Bourgh's welfare; and he could not rid himself of the disturbing apprehension that George Wynnewood was not to be trusted. If he meant to protect her, he must act quickly. Were his suspicions correct, she must be undeceived without delay. She had known George Wynnewood but a short while, and her attachment to him, however tender, could not be very deep-rooted. Though doubtless she would be grieved to find out the truth now, how much more deeply would it grieve her to make that discovery after they were wed—when the bond between them would be indissoluble?

Mrs Collins, too, felt a great interest in Anne de Bourgh's welfare; greater, perhaps, than she could well have explained; but certainly there was something to admire in a young woman who, having been brought up in all the grandeur and insolence of Rosings Park, nonetheless retained an artlessness and generosity of character wholly unlike that of her imperious mother. It could not be denied that Mr Wynnewood, in a very short time, had brought a great deal of pleasure into Miss de Bourgh's life; and if he were indeed all that he seemed, there was every reason to consider it a most auspicious match for her.

That their acquaintance was a slight one was, in Mrs

Collins' view, no impediment to their future happiness—for
she had often said of marriage, that it was better to know as
little as possible beforehand of the defects of the person with
whom you were to pass your life. Having herself married
Mr Collins upon this principle, she might by now be expected to feel some uncertainty as to the wisdom of it; but
however much she may have wished for another sort of
husband than the one she had got, the fact was that no gentleman superior to Mr Collins had ever made her an offer.
Her marriage afforded her a comfortable home, a respectable position—and her dear little boy. Given the alternative,
she did not repent it.

Miss de Bourgh's circumstances, however, were altogether different from her own. She was an heiress; and an
heiress, even a plain one, would always have eligible offers.
That Miss de Bourgh had received none before now, was
due only to the seclusion in which she had been living. It
was therefore of the greatest importance that she should not
commit herself until she had been first assured of the
gentleman's social and financial position. Mrs Collins was in
daily expectation of the letter from her mother, which
would enlighten them as to the state of Mr Wynnewood's
affairs. For Miss de Bourgh's sake, she hoped the report
would be favourable; but whatever its substance, she hoped
it would arrive soon.

~

The anticipated letter from Lady Lucas in fact arrived
the very next morning. As soon as she was up and dressed,
Anne had gone at once to her mother to make known her
engagement, and had obtained her unqualified approbation
for the match. Feeling she had rather be out of the way
when Mrs Wynnewood came to talk over the wedding
arrangements with Lady Catherine, and not expecting to see
her lover until later that afternoon, she went out with Mrs
Jenkinson after breakfast, to do some shopping in Milsom

Street. Mr Collins was, as usual, closeted upstairs with her ladyship; so, when the post was delivered, his wife was alone in the drawing room, composing a letter to her sister Maria, who had been married the previous autumn. Quickly setting aside her own letter to examine those which the footman brought in to her, and recognising her mother's handwriting on one of the packets, she immediately opened it, and read:

My dear Charlotte,

I hope this finds you and Mr Collins quite well. Your darling boy is in excellent health and spirits, though asking me every day where Mama is, and when he will be going home again. Do not be anxious that he is unhappy, however, as he is very well entertained: his grandpapa has been teaching him his alphabet, and making him paper ships to sail on the little fishpond, and riding him about the neighbourhood on the old chestnut mare, when the weather is fine. His aunts and uncles pet him, and play hide-and-seek with him, and take turns reading him a story every night at bedtime. Yesterday, Isabelle cut up bits of different coloured ribbons and tied them in little bows all through his hair. When Willy saw himself in the glass, he was so delighted that he would not have the bows taken out, and slept in them all night! So you see we do our best to amuse him, and keep him from missing his mama and papa too much.

You asked me in your last to enquire of Mrs G, whether she knew anything about the gentleman who is courting Miss de Bourgh. I called on her this morning, and found she was indeed well-acquainted with the family in question; in fact, she very recently had a letter from her sister in Cumberland, which contained a good deal of matter concerning them; and I am sorry to have to report to you, that their circumstances are anything but prosperous. Though young Mr W did inherit, on his father's death, a great fortune & a large property, the estate is now much reduced from what it was then—timber cut, acreage sold off, tenants neglected, house in disrepair, &c., &c. The village has seen little of the gentleman these ten years past, as he spends most of his time in London; it is generally known that he is an habitual gamester, and has lost enormous sums by that means. About a month ago, he returned to the country for the first time in two years; shortly thereafter, the entire family left Cumberland, to go no one knew where, just before an execution was put into their house. It was assumed by all the neighbourhood that they had probably fled to the Continent—Mrs G said the news of their being only gone to Bath would be of the greatest interest to her sister, and indeed to everyone in their village, and said she intended to write her of it as soon as I left.

I suppose the young man must have been hoping to recover his fortune by marrying well —

Charlotte had got thus far in her reading, when Mr Collins entered the drawing room.

"My dear," said he, "have you some paper and a pen here? Her ladyship wishes to dictate a letter to her steward, and—"

"That letter will have to wait, Mr Collins," said Charlotte, "for here is another just arrived, which for the moment must take precedence over any other."

Now, Mr Collins was not the most perceptive of husbands, but he was genuinely fond of his young son; and observing then the uncommon expression of gravity on his wife's countenance, and also recognising the handwriting of Lady Lucas on the sheet Charlotte was holding, he was at once roused to anxiety on William's account.

"I trust," cried he, "there is nothing amiss with the

boy?"

"No, indeed," she hastened to relieve him. "Willy is perfectly well. This letter concerns Miss de Bourgh."

"Miss de Bourgh!" he exclaimed in amazement. "What could my respected mother possibly have to communicate, that could be of any consequence to Miss de Bourgh?"

In answer, Charlotte handed him the letter to read for himself; and numerous ejaculations of surprise and dismay escaped him as he quickly perused it. When he had finished reading, he looked back at Charlotte with an expression of alarm.

"Surely," said he, "this can be naught but a shameful—a scandalous falsehood! I cannot doubt but that some villain has circulated this malicious slander, in attempt to blacken the gentleman's good name!"

"I am afraid, Mr Collins, the accusation must be true. I have known Mrs Goulding all my life, and she is not a person given to repeating mere hearsay as fact. I am satisfied she has her information on good authority."

"But my dear Charlotte! If it is as you say—what is to be done? How are we to proceed? How is the news to be broken to poor Miss de Bourgh? And—Heaven bless me!— how are we to tell her ladyship?!"

"*You* must tell Lady Catherine, Mr Collins. And leave it to me to tell Miss de Bourgh."

Mr Collins looked as if he had rather face a hangman's rope, than be obliged to carry such evil tidings to her ladyship; and for a moment Charlotte feared all his oratorical genius would be unequal to the task of communicating this one piece of news. After a little reflection, however, and in a voice of feigned composure, he said,

"Not for the first time am I now to observe, that the carrying out of such unpleasant duties as this, not infrequently devolves upon the clergyman; and I hope I will be ever ready to perform for my honourable patroness all those services for which, both by my education, and by my deep veneration for her esteemed self, I conceive myself to be peculiarly fitted. Indeed, I flatter myself I shall be able to divulge this unhappy intelligence with the utmost tact and delicacy; and I cannot but think I will readily find the words with which to provide that comfort and solace necessary, to assist her ladyship in bearing with this heavy affliction. And, by these means, I hope I may shew myself not unworthy the condescension and patronage she has always so graciously bestowed upon me."

Charlotte encouraged him with a few well-chosen words along similar lines, and before long saw her husband go off, firm in his resolve to fulfill his obligation to his revered patroness. She was then at leisure to ponder the more painful question of how she would break the news to Miss de Bourgh. She had but a few minutes' contemplation, however, before Mr Collins returned, looking rather shaken. He sat down and, to her surprise, said nothing; until at last she began,

"Well, Mr Collins? How did Lady Catherine react to your disclosure? Was she much distressed?"

He looked back at her blankly.

"I hope this blow may not prove detrimental to her recovery," Charlotte added after a moment. "She must have been greatly shocked."

"To be sure, my dear," said Mr Collins, recovering himself a little, "she cannot have been otherwise. Can her ladyship's grief and affliction under such a calamity be a matter of any question? For all her affectionate care, all her maternal devotion, to be confounded by such an iniquitous plot—all her solicitous hopes and plans for poor Miss de Bourgh dashed—a beloved daughter persecuted by the villainous proceedings of a pack of scoundrels and thieves! Indeed, her feelings of mortification and outrage can scarcely be imagined!"

"I think she cannot have said as much to you, however. You were scarce gone five minutes."

"Her ladyship said nothing which was not altogether consistent with that nobility of character, that exalted spirit, which I have ever come to expect from her."

"Exactly what," Mrs Collins persisted, "*did* she say?"

"In the first shock and horror of the moment—she said nothing at all."

"And when she did speak—?"

"She commanded me to leave her (though, by the bye, even in the midst of her affliction, not in the least departing from that gracious manner of affability and condescension, which has ever marked her treatment of me). We are to send the treacherous woman up the instant she arrives, and give her no hint as to the fate which awaits her."

"Goodness! I should not like to be in that lady's shoes. But I suppose she will be only getting what punishment she deserves."

Mr Collins would then have waxed eloquent on the severe retribution merited by all those who, in their vile and avaricious schemes, seek to betray the trust of the benevolent and virtuous; but hearing indications below that Mrs Wynnewood herself was just then arriving—and fearing he could not behold the she-devil without denouncing to her face (though of course in terms perfectly consistent with Christian charity) the infamous behaviour of herself and her son—he hastened away, and left his wife to encounter the enemy alone.

Mrs Collins, with her customary self-possession, walked out to meet Mrs Wynnewood as she reached the landing; and after exchanging with her the briefest of greetings, informed her Lady Catherine was awaiting her upstairs, and most anxious for her to come up without delay. Having watched the visitor ascend in ignorance of the fury in store for her, Charlotte re-entered the drawing room; whence, after a quarter-hour, she had a distinct view of the same lady flying past in great haste, as though escaping a frightful apparition, and in seeming disregard of aught save quitting the house as quickly as possible.

Chapter 13

Mrs Collins was still sitting alone in the drawing room when, much later, Anne returned with Mrs Jenkinson to Sydney Place.

Anne had given her bonnet and pelisse to one of the maids, directed a footman how to dispose of her parcels, and was about to go up to see her mother, when she heard Mrs Collins call out to her from within the drawing room—bidding her stop a moment, as she had a matter of some importance to discuss with her.

After Anne had come in and seated herself, Charlotte began, "I have some rather unhappy news to report to you, Miss de Bourgh."

"I hope my mother is no worse?" said Anne.

"No; my news concerns Mr Wynnewood."

"Mr Wynnewood?"

Charlotte hesitated a moment before proceeding. "I am very sorry to have to tell you," she said, "that Mr Wynnewood's—situation—is not what we thought it was."

"His situation? What do you mean, Mrs Collins? I do not understand."

There was another slight pause as Charlotte weighed her words. "You believe Mr Wynnewood to be a rich man," said she, "do you not?"

Anne gave a little laugh at the foolishness of such a question. "Why, of course he is rich; he has told me so himself. That is, he has spoken to me of matters, which make it plain he is a gentleman of very large fortune."

Mrs Collins' reply was straightforward, though kindly

spoken. "He has misled you, Miss de Bourgh. I have learned only this morning that Mr Wynnewood is by no means a wealthy man; that he is, in fact—a bankrupt."

Anne was silent for a moment; then she gave another little laugh and, shaking her head, said, "My dear Mrs Collins, that is impossible. It cannot be."

With a solemn countenance, Charlotte handed her Lady Lucas's letter, and pointed to the relevant passage. Anne obediently read; but continued, as she did so, to shake her head in disbelief.

"This cannot be true." She handed the letter back. "Lady Lucas's friend must be misinformed; or she has misinformed Lady Lucas. When Mr Wynnewood comes to dinner today, I am sure he will be able to explain it all."

"I do not believe Mr Wynnewood will be coming to dinner," said Charlotte, gently but firmly, "today, or any other day. I do not believe you will see anything more of the Wynnewoods."

Anne pressed a hand to her breast. "Mrs Wynnewood was to call on my mother this morning—"

"She has come, and gone. Lady Catherine sent her away."

"But—Mr Wynnewood and I are to be married; my mother gave her consent to the match but a few hours ago! Mrs Wynnewood is her old friend—"

"They are friends no longer, Miss de Bourgh."

"And the captain—" (snatching at the smallest mite of hope) "I know you think well of the captain. His intimacy with Mr Wynnewood is of many years' continuance. Surely you don't believe *he* could be so wholly deceived in Mr Wynnewood's character?"

"They have only recently renewed their acquaintance; it is quite possible, therefore, that the captain is unaware of Mr Wynnewood's circumstances."

"No!" she cried, "It is all a mistake—a horrible, dreadful mistake!"

Tears stung at her eyes. She would not believe it! It

was a lie—or an error—she would prove it was so! She would go to the South Parade at once—she would find George—she would ask him directly!

She jumped up and rushed from the room, down the stairs and out through the front door of the house, heedless of Mrs Collins calling after her, heedless of the servant watching her in astonishment, heedless of the cold, heedless of anything at all; until, after darting down the front steps, she ran headlong into the very solid impediment of Captain Turner at the bottom of them.

"Miss de Bourgh!" he exclaimed, steadying her with both hands, as she appeared in some danger of falling over. "I beg your pardon—"

Not even endeavouring to conceal her agitation, she cried, "Pray excuse me. I cannot speak to you now, Captain. I am on my way to the South Parade. I must go at once. It is most urgent—"

Shocked to see her so distraught, he said, "I have just come from the South Parade myself. You will not find either Miss Wynnewood or her brother there—if that is your object."

"If they are out, I shall wait for them until they return."

He looked at her with a mixture of pity and concern. "It will do you no good, Miss de Bourgh. They are gone."

"Gone? But surely, they will be back before—"

"I am afraid they will not be back," he said very gently. "They have left Bath.—But it is very cold today, and you have no coat; will you not go back inside with me now, and—"

"No, you are wrong!" she cried in desperation, almost overcome with the conviction that Mr Wynnewood had indeed deceived her. "You must have misunderstood. They are gone, perhaps, to call on friends in some other part of town—"

"If you will but go back inside with me now, Miss de Bourgh, I should be happy to explain to you—"

"They may have driven out to Clifton for the day," she suggested, though speaking now in a tone almost of hopelessness. "Or perhaps over to Wick Rocks."

"Miss de Bourgh, I am very sorry to cause you pain— more sorry than I can express; but you would know the truth soon enough, in any case. I promise you, I will tell you all I know; but I must entreat you again, to go back inside before you take cold."

He held out his arm to her. After a few moments' private struggle, she finally took it, with an air of resignation; and together they returned into the house. Inside they were met by Mrs Collins, who had been observing them through a window in the dining room, and came out into the hall as they entered. Silently, she led them to the back parlour where, she considered, they would be less in danger of intrusion.

When they were all three seated together, there was a little pause before Anne, in a disconsolate tone, said to the captain,

"Then it is all, I suppose, as Mrs Collins has told me? Mr Wynnewood is really a—a pauper?"

He nodded gravely.

"But if you knew what he was, Captain—why did you not tell me, before I had—?"

He protested he had not known, though he had suspected. He enumerated for her the circumstances that had roused his mistrust: the horses, the habit, the boots, the carriage wheel. When he got to the most damning evidence— the one hundred pounds—Anne was dumbfounded. George Wynnewood had shamelessly gambled away one hundred pounds of the captain's meagre funds, and then laughed at him for giving a trifle to help Mr Gower!

"But as you may imagine," the captain continued, "I did not like to accuse my old friend without indisputable proof. After what had taken place between you yesterday, however—or rather," he amended hastily, "what I guessed had taken place—I resolved to confront him this morning with my misgivings, and give him a chance to remove them if he could.

"With that object in mind I went today to the South Parade; it was the housekeeper who told me the family had left Bath. I pressed her to give me what information she could, and found her more than willing to oblige me. Mrs Wynnewood, she said, had gone out earlier in the morning—"

"She came here to call on Lady Catherine," Charlotte interposed, "and received her dismissal."

"Well, it seems she returned home a short time later, in a very great perturbation. She at once summoned her son and daughter together, and the three of them packed up all their belongings in the greatest haste. Within the hour they had departed in a hackney coach."

Here he paused; and Anne, observing the unhappiness in his eyes at that moment, mistook the cause of that unhappiness, and recollected she was not the only one whose heart was broken. Of course the captain loved Louisa, as she loved George. Grieving for her own loss, her heart swelled with compassion for his.

"The housekeeper further told me," he continued, "that not half an hour after they vacated the house, the bailiffs arrived to arrest George Wynnewood, for debts amounting to more than twenty thousand pounds."

At this revelation, Anne gasped in shock and dismay; and "Heaven forbid!" and "Poor George!" were her tender interjections.

"And now, Miss de Bourgh," he concluded with a heavy sigh, "I believe you know quite as much about this unfortunate affair, as I know myself."

She was lost in silent reflection for a short while; then, "And—you are really perfectly convinced, Captain, of the truth of this story? You are quite certain the housekeeper is to be trusted?"

"I have not the smallest doubt of it."

There was little more to be said; and Captain Turner

took his leave of them soon afterward. Anne then excused herself, begging Mrs Collins to explain everything to Mrs Jenkinson, and went upstairs to her bedchamber. On the way she passed by her mother's door, and stopped a moment, feeling she ought to go in. No doubt Lady Catherine would wish to speak to her about this painful misadventure; but she could not face Lady Catherine just yet. She walked on until she had gained her own room and, closing the door behind her, lay down upon her bed and wept.

Chapter 14

Some time later, having at last done crying (save for a little hiccuping sob which from time to time escaped her), Anne found herself listening to every sound which rose from below with a kind of irrational half-expectancy that the Wynnewoods might yet appear; but hearing nothing to herald their arrival, she could not bring herself to go down to dinner. Mrs Collins, however, thoughtfully ordered a tray to be brought up to her; and despite that total want of appetite, which she had at first believed herself to feel—and which would certainly have been requisite for any true heroine, suffering under so severe a disappointment—Anne managed at length to consume a bowl of pease soup, a slice of beef, two buttered rolls, and a small apple tart. And though she did not waken in the morning with any happier reflections than those she had gone to bed with, she did, in perfect disregard of what was owed to sensibility, sleep through the night quite soundly.

With a sense of duty, but with no great eagerness, Anne early repaired to her mother's room on the following morning. Lady Catherine was energetic on the subject of the Wynnewoods' treachery. Indeed, her indignation seemed almost to have restored her to her accustomed vigor. "She was shocked and outraged at the infamous conduct of all three—had never in her life encountered such ingratitude— and after such trust and friendship as she had favoured them with! She could not have imagined such a pack of hardened villains to exist in all of England. Mr Wynnewood was a scoundrel, his mother a viper, his sister—even worse.

They had used her and her daughter abominably ill, and she hoped they would reap their just deserts."

The old governess, too, came in for a share of her censure. "She was greatly displeased with Mrs Jenkinson, who ought to have taken better care of Anne; she was not looking after her as she should. Had she herself been well, this could not have happened. She was excessively attentive to all such matters, and should very soon have caught the Wynnewoods out in their scheming."

Though with little enough spirit to respond otherwise to Lady Catherine's tirade, Anne here felt compelled to intercede on her elderly companion's behalf.

"I cannot think Mrs Jenkinson so much to blame, ma'am," said she. "You spent a great deal of time with Mrs Wynnewood, and yet did not detect anything untoward in her conduct."

"Yes, but I was not myself," Lady Catherine replied in a tone of vexation. "Had I been in health, I should certainly have seen through her charade. As it is, we are indebted to Mrs Collins for your deliverance; and you may be sure Mrs Jenkinson will receive a strong reprimand from me, for her part in the affair.

"Furthermore, Anne," she continued, "you are not to repine over that worthless young man; you are well rid of him. When I am recovered, I shall find you a husband myself—one befitting the daughter of Sir Lewis de Bourgh, and the heiress of Rosings Park."

Her daughter making no reply, Lady Catherine closed by saying, "If you are going down to breakfast now, you may tell Mrs Jenkinson I wish to speak to her."

Anne might have resented her mother's insensitive remarks, had she not been feeling so depressed; as it was, they only served to depress her the more. She sighed, and left Lady Catherine to the full enjoyment of her wrath. Descending the stairs to the dining room, she met Mrs Jenkinson coming up.

"Oh! Miss de Bourgh," cried that lady, "What a terrible business this is! Mrs Collins told me all. I am very much afraid your health will suffer by it. Indeed, you look quite knocked up; I fear you did not sleep last night. Directly you have had your breakfast, I would entreat you to lie down and rest. And perhaps tomorrow you had better go into the hot bath. Do not you think you ought? I really am very much concerned."

While owning to some feeling of lassitude, Anne assured the old woman she had slept quite well, and did not feel in any danger of falling into a fever. She then delivered her mother's message, and saw a look of guilt and alarm overspread Mrs Jenkinson's countenance. Knowing there was naught she could do to protect her companion from Lady Catherine's ire, she only gave her a wan smile of encouragement, and, by way of compensation for the abuse she was about to endure, expressed her willingness to submit to visiting the baths on the morrow.

Mr and Mrs Collins were seated together at the table when Anne entered the dining parlour a few moments later. Seeing her, Mr Collins leapt from his chair and assailed her with a torrent of sympathy, gripping both her hands between his own as he poured forth his eloquent solace. Words were insufficient to express his sense of outrage over the barbarous treatment she had received at the hands of Mr Wynnewood and his family; and he could not satisfy himself without denouncing their conduct at great length. He dwelt, too, with all his usual delicacy, on the piteousness of her situation—how, sadly, at her time of life, this shocking affair must destroy any hopes of her ever being married— how unlikely it was, that she would ever recover from so severe a disappointment.

"Moreover, Miss de Bourgh," said he, "I cannot doubt but that her ladyship, already reduced by her injuries to a state of extreme debility, will sink into a precipitous decline, as a result of this evil perpetrated against a daughter so beloved, and expire from her grief." Allowing her a few moments to contemplate the full horror of this prospect, he then added, "I would exhort you to be consoled, however, in the certainty that this humiliating contretemps is at present known to no one but ourselves; together, of course, with Captain Turner—and doubtless every servant in the house; as well as Lady Lucas, Mrs Goulding, and Mrs Goulding's sister—besides, probably, *their* most intimate friends, and perhaps some few of their neighbours. You may likewise take comfort, my dear Miss de Bourgh, in the conviction that you have done nothing yourself to invite this despicable treachery. Indeed, I am inclined to believe that Mr Wynnewood and all his family are so irredeemably wicked that, had any other young woman equally rich, and equally credulous, fallen in their way, she would surely have suffered the same doleful fate as yourself."

Though Miss de Bourgh did not appear to receive from this soothing elocution all the comfort he intended, Mr Collins would have prolonged it, had not his wife reminded him of a commission he had undertaken to perform for her in town that morning. With one last squeeze of Miss de Bourgh's hands, therefore, and one final pitying glance at her, he took his leave, and hastened away.

Anne was soon provided with breakfast from the sideboard; and having dismissed the servant, she began rather tremulously, "I have not yet thanked you, Mrs Collins, for the pains you took to discover Mr Wynnewood's real circumstances—and for the kindness you showed in communicating them to me."

"I was very sorry indeed," said Charlotte with a sympathising smile, "to have to relate anything so unpleasant to you; but once I knew the truth myself, I could not allow you to remain in ignorance. Had he once got hold of your fortune, Mr Wynnewood would certainly have ruined you. But plainly," she added, "you have a superfluity of friends ready to tell you their feelings on this subject. If you have any need of a friend to listen rather than talk, however—you may be sure I would regard it as a compliment to be honoured with your confidence."

"You are very kind," Anne responded. She began then to speak aloud what had been in her thoughts since the disclosures of the previous day. "It was foolish in me ever to have thought of marrying," she said. "That I should have imagined myself capable, at my age, and with so little claim to beauty, of exciting real affection in any man worth having—! But I am better off as I am. Indeed, I am much more fortunate than many, for I need never worry how I shall keep myself. I will never want for anything. Except—"

"Except?"

"I should so much have liked to find someone—on whom I might have bestowed my affection. I know it is very wrong in me, to be dissatisfied with my lot; yet the thought of going back to Rosings, back to my old life, just as if nothing were changed, is hard to bear. Mr Wynnewood has greatly injured me; but at the same time, he has shown me clearly how deficient was my former mode of living."

"But though you return to Rosings, you need not go back to exactly the same mode of living, I suppose? Nor need you yet despair, I think, of making a satisfactory match. I had quite given up hope of marrying, you know, before I met Mr Collins."

"Yes, but—" Anne stopped short. She could not tell Charlotte she had rather remain a spinster than be wed to such a man as Mr Collins. Charlotte understood her, however; and replied, with a smile and a very faint blush,

"But perhaps you feel a man like Mr Collins would not suit you? For I am sure you have often wondered at my having accepted him myself."

Anne opened her lips to offer a polite equivocation, but before she could speak Charlotte continued,

"I will tell you candidly, Miss de Bourgh, that though I never did feel for Mr Collins that romantic sort of attachment one so often reads about, neither did I ever expect to feel, or to inspire, such a sentiment. I wished only a respectable and secure provision for the future; and my marriage to Mr Collins has more than answered my views on that score."

"But—you are fond of him?"

"He is my husband. Yes, in my own way, I suppose I am fond of him. And indeed, perhaps I like him the better for that resemblance in character which I have often observed, between him and my dear father."

"I have had the pleasure of meeting Sir William Lucas," said Anne, "when he has visited you at Hunsford; and I hope you will forgive my saying, that I have never remarked the smallest likeness between them myself. Mr Collins—talks a great deal; while Sir William Lucas hardly speaks at all."

Charlotte smiled. "Ah, but that is only when he is in the presence of Lady Catherine de Bourgh, of whose dignity and consequence he stands in very great awe. But in less exalted company, I assure you he is every bit as talkative as Mr Collins is.

"To own the truth, Miss de Bourgh," she went on after a moment, "they are neither of them what is commonly referred to as—men of talents. But they are both good husbands (if to treat one's wife with consideration and respect is to be a good husband)—and affectionate fathers. I never looked for more. And even if my design in marrying had been to provide myself an object to dote upon, I have accomplished that end as well—in my dear little William."

"Oh! he is indeed a sweet child."

Despite the sweetness of young William Collins, Anne could not feel that she would ever have acted as Charlotte had done. Conscious, however, of the differences between them, both in temper and situation, she was rather pleased with the friendship betokened by this frank explanation. She did not pity Charlotte so much as she had done, and respected her a good deal more.

Later that morning, Captain Turner called to enquire after Anne, and she received him in the drawing room in the presence of Mrs Collins and Mrs Jenkinson, with a composed, but certainly not a cheerful demeanour. After a few awkward commonplaces had been exchanged, he remarked that the weather was considerably milder than it had been on the previous day, and wondered if Miss de Bourgh would do him the honour of accompanying him on a walk through the Gardens; desiring, of course, that Mrs Collins and Mrs Jenkinson would both consent to join them.

Anne felt little inclination to accept his invitation; and Mrs Jenkinson, with Lady Catherine's stinging reproofs fresh in her mind, tendered some strong objections in consideration of Miss de Bourgh's health. The captain, however, assured her that the morning air was quite warm and dry, and could in no way affect Miss de Bourgh's health but for the better. He then appealed to Mrs Collins, who hesitated not to express her own opinion that Miss de Bourgh would find refreshment in a little air and exercise, as well as a change of scene; and Anne was soon persuaded.

Captain Turner walked beside her, with the other two ladies following behind them, as they went across to the Gardens. There was at first no conversation between them, Anne's thoughts being much taken up with the remembrance of their last such outing, made in the company of Mr Wynnewood and his sister. To end the silence, the captain began talking of a letter he had just received from his brother, announcing the birth of that gentleman's third child, a little girl. He related his own delight in the news, and went on to speak with affection of his other nieces and nephews (he had six more, besides this infant), telling Anne all their names and ages, relating some little anecdotes of their childish antics, and repeating some of their comical utterances for her amusement.

"I suppose, Captain," said she in a desponding tone, "you will have children of your own someday."

"I hope I will," said he.

Yes—he might have lost Louisa; but he would find another, and love again. Anne could entertain no such hope for herself.

Absorbed in their separate musings, neither spoke

again for some time; when she asked abruptly, "Do you think, Captain Turner—do you think Mr Wynnewood cared for me at all?"

Whatever his true opinion of the matter, he readily replied, "I am sure that he did."

Anne was only briefly cheered by this avowal. After a little pause to reflect, she shook her head. "Had he been genuinely attached to me, he would have asked me to marry him in spite of my mother's disapproval. He would have begged me to give up my fortune, that we might be together."

"But—would you have been willing to make such a sacrifice, Miss de Bourgh?"

"Yes. Yes, I think I would."

He seemed occupied in deep contemplation for a little time; then he said, "George Wynnewood's circumstances were very bad, however. It could not have been in his power to marry without some attention to money."

"He once told me," said she, "he believed in marrying only for love."

After another little pause, she concluded with a sigh, "But it was all falsehood, from beginning to end. I am persuaded he never cared for me at all."

Chapter 15

Lady Catherine soon decided it was time for Mr Collins to return to Hunsford. She was greatly concerned that his parishioners would be getting into trouble, with neither herself nor him (as her deputy) to keep them out of mischief. The clergyman whom Mr Collins had appointed to perform his duties in his absence might do well enough at delivering the sermons, and conducting the necessary rites; but he would not know that Tim Lincoln must be kept from beating his apprentices—that Jed Bragg must be stopped from getting drunk every Saturday, and quarreling with his wife—or that, if old Martha Stokes were not made to accept the charity of her neighbours, she would starve.

No—Mr Collins's presence was required at Hunsford. Lady Catherine gave *Mrs* Collins permission to remain, however, to oversee the domestic business of Sydney Place. Anne, thinking it unfeeling to divide Mrs Collins from her child any longer, interceded on Charlotte's behalf; and her ladyship graciously consented to allow little William Collins to be sent for, to bide with his mother for the remainder of her residence in Bath. The substitution of young William for his father was an exchange to gratify all concerned, excepting perhaps Mr Collins himself—who, if he was no more to enjoy the felicity of serving her ladyship in Sydney Place, might have preferred to bring his wife and son back to Hunsford with him. But Lady Catherine's wish was ever his command, and whatever his private vexation, he promptly obeyed.

Captain Turner called frequently at Sydney Place in

the days that followed. When the weather was fine, he and Anne walked across to the Gardens, accompanied by Mrs Jenkinson, or by Mrs Collins and her son, or more commonly by all three. He diverted them with accounts of the remarkable places he had been (for in the course of his naval career he had travelled to both the East Indies and the West, and all around Africa and the Levant) and he related to them the strange legends and customs of some of the foreign tribes and races he had encountered over the years. He quickly became a favourite with little William, who thrilled to his stories of battles, storms, and shipwrecks, and whose lively play he delighted to share.

He also talked to Anne of his friends the Gowers, to whom she had previously shown such generosity. Their circumstances were now in every way improved: thanks to the skill of the surgeon sent to attend her, and the wholesome diet which had been provided her, Mrs Gower was almost well again. Her husband, too, had the promise of employment in America, where his son had been established for some years as a chandler, and had lately realised a fair profit in that concern. The young man had written, urging his parents to emigrate, and had even sent the money for their passage; they expected to sail within the fortnight. Through the captain, they begged leave to call at Sydney Place before they left, to pay their respects and offer their thanks to the lady whose goodness had relieved their distress. Anne, with disagreeable recollections of Lady Catherine's haughty condescension to the abject recipients of her alms, demurred, but sent back a friendly message wishing them every happiness in their new home.

She was exceedingly grateful for Captain Turner's many kind attentions towards her. Though George Wynnewood's name was never mentioned between them, she could not doubt but that he meant, by his interesting talk, to distract her from dwelling too much on that gentleman's desertion. She was the more grateful when she considered how much he must be suffering himself, in the loss of

Louisa; but he was now quite recovered from the injury which had brought him to Bath, and awaited only a posting into another ship to return to active service. Once immersed again in his former way of life, she believed, the need to focus his energies on the effective discharge of his duties must greatly assist him in forgetting his sorrow. There would be no such consolation for her.

In March, all England was electrified by the news of Napoleon's escape from Elba. Captain Turner, to his joy, was promptly given command of a frigate, the 32-gun *Veritas*, and ordered to report to Portsmouth without delay. Before his departure, however, he called once more in Sydney Place to take a final walk in the Gardens with Anne, and to bid her and her friends farewell.

"Will you be staying in Bath much longer yourself, Miss de Bourgh?" he asked as they strolled together along the canal. Mrs Collins and her son had accompanied them on the outing, but were now lagging a little behind.

"I hardly know. My mother is eager to return to Rosings as soon as possible, but at present she is not fit to travel. As soon as she is sufficiently recovered, I imagine we shall be gone directly."

"And may I dare to hope—" he began hesitantly, "May I dare to hope that, when you are home again in Kent, you will also begin to recover—from your disappointment? The wound is yet too fresh, I know; but in time, I trust—"

He trailed off without completing the thought. Anne gave him a mournful smile, and sighed; and a brief silence ensued before she ventured,

"And may I trust you will have so much to occupy you in your new office, Captain—that you will soon forget your own disappointment?"

"My own—?" he asked in some confusion.

"As to Louisa—that is, Miss Wynnewood."

"I am afraid," said he, "I do not understand you."

With a trace of archness unusual in her, she replied, "Do you not?"

"Oh! Do you mean—? Did you think I was—in love with Miss Wynnewood? I never was."

Anne looked her surprise, and he admitted, "I did think her very beautiful at one time. But I soon found there was not much else there to interest me. No, it is not Miss Wynnewood I will be thinking of—"

"Of course," she promptly concluded with another smile. Not for the world would she make him confess an attachment which, plainly, he would rather forget. "You will be dreaming only of the next battle—of the prizes you shall capture, and the honours you shall win."

After a moment, she added more seriously, "I pray God will keep you safe, Captain—and grant you victory in every endeavour."

~

Once Lady Catherine was sufficiently mended to make travel practicable, she was impatient to be at home; and before word reached England of Wellington's great triumph at Waterloo (a triumph, however, in which many thousands of gallant soldiers, even among the allied forces, lost their lives) Anne and her mother, along with Mrs Collins, little William, and Mrs Jenkinson, had returned to Kent. At first, her ladyship was confined to a wheeled chair, and required to have someone always at hand to push her about in it—an office Mr Collins took upon himself with great zeal, whenever he could persuade the footman who usually performed the duty to relinquish it. Eventually she progressed to the use of crutches, and then to a cane; making sure, of course, that the latter was of the richest and most elegant design. She consoled herself for the permanent diminishment of her mobility with this cheering reflection: that the judicious brandishing of her cane rendered her a still more formidable object to her inferiors, than she had ever been before.

The intimacy between Anne and Charlotte Collins, formed at Bath, continued and flourished. With Charlotte's private encouragement (for, had Mr Collins known of her interference, it would surely have been a source of contention between him and his wife) Anne acquired a horse and began riding every day. She also began making charitable visits to the poor cottages in the neighbourhood. She engaged an array of masters to tutor her, if belatedly, in music, dancing, and drawing; and even requested Charlotte to instruct her in the rudiments of household management.

After voicing some few trifling objections, Lady Catherine, much to her daughter's astonishment, wisely gave her blessing to all these measures. She could not but see that Anne's health was much improved of late, nor could she fail to perceive that Anne had lately shown a good deal more spirit than she had previously given her credit for; and she was secretly pleased at the alteration. Her ladyship at first continued firm in her resolve to find her daughter a suitable husband; and she did make some fresh attempts in that direction, after they returned to Rosings. But as fitting candidates for so great an honour were few and far between— and as Anne herself evinced little interest in the project, and still less in the particular aspirants presented for her consideration—after a time her ladyship slackened in her efforts, and to all intents and purposes gave up the search.

In Charlotte Collins, Anne found the sympathetic listener and friend she had long desired; and Charlotte was well-pleased to have secured for herself the companionship and conversation of someone who was not Mr Collins. Anne often talked with Charlotte of Bath, and of Mr Wynnewood and his sister. She also talked of Captain Turner from time to time—and thought of him, and of his kindness to her, a good deal more. Charlotte obtained for her a copy of the Navy List, and together they looked up his ships, the *Defiance*, the *Amphitrite* and his present one, the *Veritas*. Though the war with France was ended, pirates yet roamed the seas; and to His Majesty's navy fell the perilous task of routing out these murderous enemies to commerce. Thus Anne got into a regular habit of perusing the newspaper, that she might know whenever the *Veritas* had been engaged in any actions; and she was always gratified to find no 'Captain Samuel Turner' among the names of the dead.

Chapter 16

One day in June, about a year after she left Bath, Anne was sitting alone at the far end of the rose garden at Rosings Park, an unopened book beside her on the garden bench. She had come out with the intention of reading, but after a time had put her book aside, and now sat idly musing, enjoying the warmth of the sun, and the lush fragrance of the roses.

On balance, her reflections were more than satisfactory. She had long since ceased to regret Mr Wynnewood, having finally assured herself he had loved not her, but her fortune; and having consequently and quite rightly concluded, that their marriage, had it been accomplished, could never have been a happy one. Moreover, she had learned from that overthrow of her hopes, no longer to fix those hopes on illusory dreams of love, but to content herself with actual circumstances which, if less than perfect, were no bad lot; and to seek, within their limits, to do as much good for others, and to bring as much happiness to herself, as was within her capacity. She had now many sources of enjoyment open to her, which had been previously outside her sphere; and her friendship with Charlotte Collins, and her affection for little William, added some sweetness to her existence—though perhaps not so much as she might have found, had she been blessed with a husband and children of her own.

In the midst of these mostly agreeable musings, she was surprised by the sight of a gentleman in a dark blue coat, walking towards her along the garden path. With feelings half confusion and half delight, she stood and walked forward to meet him, smiling and holding out her hand. She was not only surprised to see him, but surprised by what she saw. She had been remembering him this twelvemonth as a somewhat ill-featured gentleman, though not really unpleasant-looking. But now he stood before her, appearing, if not precisely handsome, very nearly so. How odd that he should be so altered!

"Captain Turner," she said, as he took her hand and bowed over it. "I am very glad to see you. What brings you into Kent?"

"The *Veritas*—my ship—was damaged in a storm a short while ago, and is hove down for repairs in Portsmouth. I put my lieutenant in charge of directing the repairs for a few days, that I might come and—pay my respects to you. The servant told me I should find you out here."

He then enquired politely after her health, and after her mother, and the Collinses, and Mrs Jenkinson; and had the satisfaction of hearing that they were all very well indeed. There was an embarrassed pause; then,

"Will you come inside, Captain," Anne suggested, "and take some refreshment? I am expecting Mrs Collins shortly, and—"

"No—thank you. I had rather stay here, in the garden—if you would grant me the honour of—. That is to say—if you would allow me—there was something particular I wished to speak to you about."

Whereupon they sat together on the garden bench, with the roses blooming all about them; and, in language wholly fitting, if hardly poetic, he told her that he loved her: that he had loved her before they parted at Bath—had loved her these twelve months past.

He spoke at even greater length of misgivings which had cost him many an hour of troubled reflection; of her superiority in fortune and connections, and of his own scruples regarding that inequality between them, which had nearly prevented him making any confession of his feelings.

Even now, he said, he doubted whether he was not acting dishonourably in addressing her. But he had learned through hard experience that a man can gain nothing he desires in life, if he will not sometimes try for what is beyond his grasp. So he asked her plainly: Could she return his affection? — Would she consent to be his wife?

The captain's declaration of love surprised Anne, though not at first disagreeably. But in dwelling subsequently on her superiority of fortune, &c., he expressed himself unluckily. He had felt it necessary, as a point of honour, to acknowledge the inferiority of his situation as compared to her own; but his according the subject so much importance only served to raise in her a suspicion that material considerations, rather than real attachment, prompted his proposal. He seemed suddenly a second George Wynnewood, who sought her hand only to secure her fortune. With disappointment and displeasure in her breast, she said,

"I had not expected this of you, Captain — you of all people. Knowing as you do, how deeply I was hurt by Mr Wynnewood — I think you might have spared me this. You are not aware, I suppose, that I have hardly any fortune which is not bestowed at my mother's pleasure; and you may be sure, sir, that were I to marry you, she would give me nothing. So you see, you need not have bothered to disturb my tranquillity — "

"You quite mistake me!" he exclaimed with a mingled air of unhappiness and offended pride. "Indeed, you mistake me altogether. I care nothing for your fortune, Miss de Bourgh. Your mother may do as she likes with her money — she may give it all to — to the the missionaries of Boggley-Wollah*, as far as I am concerned! In bestowing yourself, you would bestow everything I care for. I am not rich; but neither am I a beggar — or a knave. I would ask for no woman's hand, if I could not offer my whole heart in return."

Anne wavered. She had always believed him an honourable man. He had always been kind to her. Still — she had been duped once; she would not be duped again.

"But you *are* very poor, Captain—are you not?"

With some asperity, he replied, "Yes. Yes, I suppose I am very poor—by comparison with the heiress of Rosings Park. But I am not destitute. I have a small property near Portsmouth, left me by my father; and the money I have won by my profession—amounting, now, to some ten thousand pounds, with at least the hope of more in future. I ought to have waited for more, perhaps; but I feared to lose my chance if I did—these are not promising times for sailors. To marry me would be a very great condescension on your part, to be sure. But if you could—" (here his tone changed to one of ardent entreaty) "—if you could care for me enough, to lower yourself to live upon such a modest income as I can provide—I would endeavour by every means in my power to make you happy."

"I wonder, Captain," said she after a little pause, "why you did not tell me of your attachment before you left Bath?"

"I very nearly did—when I found you had mistaken my feelings for Miss Wynnewood. But you were in love with George Wynnewood; how could I ask you to think of me? I should have been disparaging the warmth of your heart to suppose you capable of so sudden a shift in your affections. However, I hoped the passage of a year or two would give you time to forget him—and might see me a little the richer besides."

When she did not immediately reply, he went on,

"I was encouraged too, by your saying you would have given up your fortune to marry him—because I could not suppose my own suit would be looked on favourably by your mother, even if I were so lucky as to gain your affections in time."

"Do you mean to say—you would wish to marry me, even without any hope of obtaining my fortune?"

"I should be ashamed to take it if it were offered."

Anne struggled to comprehend this new idea. It seemed Mr Wynnewood had misled her in so many things! Her emotions were all in a tumult as she began to consider—to imagine the possibility of accepting the captain's proposal; and she began to think that she might *wish* to accept it. She began to feel, indeed, that she *did* love him—that she had loved him for some time, without ever having realised it! From the very beginning of their acquaintance, she had felt for him a liking and esteem; she had been anxious for his welfare. When he left Bath, she had felt the loss of his friendship. And for many months since her return to Rosings, she had thought of him, and prayed for him—in truth, she had longed for him. Why had she not seen it before now? And how could she ever have believed herself in love with George Wynnewood? He was nothing. Captain Turner was everything!

After this long pause, he took up her hand in his; repeated his professions of love; and once more asked her to be his wife. Another moment elapsed before Anne, with the greatest feeling both of wonder and happiness within her, replied,

"Yes—I will. I will marry you, Captain Turner."

"You will!"

~

The man must needs have the forbearance of a saint, the courage of a soldier, and the sangfroid of a philosopher, who could contemplate, with anything like equanimity, the prospect of having Lady Catherine de Bourgh for a mother-in-law. But Captain Turner, who had braved fierce storms and fiercer battles, was not to be intimidated by the likes of Lady Catherine. And I am proud to say that even Anne, who had been wont to tremble at the mere thought of provoking her mother's anger, showed herself, on this occasion, to be truly her ladyship's own daughter. It was arranged between the two lovers that Captain Turner should, before he left Rosings, be introduced to Lady Catherine; but Anne wished to break the news of their engagement to her

mother in her own way, after he had gone; and to this stipu-
lation he reluctantly acceded.

When informed by her daughter of the betrothal she
had entered into, Lady Catherine yet again had need of all
her celebrated frankness of character; and she hesitated not
to employ it, in her attempts to dissuade Anne from so rash
a design.

"Captain Turner!" she cried, with a queenly flourish
of her walking stick. "A mere Captain Turner! And who,
pray, is Captain Turner, to be addressing Miss Anne de
Bourgh—the future mistress of Rosings Park—daughter of
Sir Lewis de Bourgh—cousin to Mr Darcy of Pemberley—
granddaughter to the eighth Earl of _____ , and niece to the
ninth? Offering ten thousand pounds, to a woman who
would inherit a fortune of twenty times that sum!

"Are you lost to all propriety and decorum, Anne?
Have you no sense of duty or obligation? Do you owe no
deference to the wishes of your family? No obedience to
your mother?

"His father a penniless tutor! His mother—what?
Perhaps the daughter of some country attorney. Turner! A
name not even of tolerable gentility! His great-grandfather, I
suppose, was a carpenter or a cabinet-maker. It surpasses
even the degradation of Darcy's alliance! When a man of
property and position stoops to marry a woman of no consequence, he at least raises her to his own rank by the
marriage; but when a woman of rank stoops to marry a
nobody, she is herself reduced to a nobody by the connection.

"A common sailor! And without even any attractions
of person, or charms of address to justify your infatuation!
Scoundrel as he was, George Wynnewood had at least that
much to offer—and pedigree as well. Captain Turner! No
elegance or refinement to compensate for his low descent, a
mere clod of a fellow. And this is the mediocrity to which
you would debase yourself. This is the legacy you would
bequeath to my grandchildren! Foolish, willful girl! De

Bourghs and Fitzwilliams have been proprietors of great manors—peers of the realm—ministers of state—bishops and judges. Your great-great-great aunt was a Mistress of the Robes—your great-great-uncle a Lord Steward of the Household! Heaven and Earth—of what can you be thinking, Anne? Is all the eminence of their blood to be defiled by such a taint?"

In response to these vituperations, Anne said very little, though her pulses throbbed, and her every limb trembled with suppressed indignation on the captain's account. But she knew it would be fruitless to try and defend her choice to Lady Catherine. She remained unwavering in her resolve, however; and, as her ladyship's mode of governance did not extend to locking her thirty-year-old daughter in her room until she could be made to see reason, Anne carried her point. Where money and patronage, or the threat of their withdrawal, could not awe, Lady Catherine was powerless to compel.

When the captain, accompanied by his mother and sister, returned to Rosings a week later to carry Anne to his home on the Hampshire coast, whence their marriage was to take place, the sword which had delivered him from many a foe was nowhere in evidence, nor was it needed: the present adversary met his incursion not with an armed resistance, but with a cold and angry silence. Anne had been watching for him, however, and had her few small trunks—she took no more away with her—already placed by the front door, in anticipation of her departure.

Before they left the house, the pair entered the drawing room so that Anne might bid farewell to her mother, perhaps forever; but Lady Catherine would deign neither to look at nor to speak to her. Mrs Jenkinson, having been forbidden to say anything on the occasion, could only dab her handkerchief at her eyes and blink mournfully at them both. The Captain made her ladyship a brief address, respectfully assuring her of his heartfelt affection for her daughter, and expressing a wish that she might in time be reconciled to their union. For his pains he received a cutting glare which would have cowed a lesser man. Vexed for Anne's sake, but not otherwise unsettled by this repulse, he bowed to Mrs Jenkinson and wished her well. Offering his arm then to his betrothed, he led her out to meet his own mother, and his sister, Caroline, who had been sitting together in the carriage anxiously awaiting their first interview with the unknown lady on whom all of their dear Samuel's future happiness would depend.

Anne de Bourgh might have forfeited a mother to wed the captain, but in doing so she acquired a new and most affectionate mother in Mrs Turner, as well as several brothers and sisters who warmly welcomed her into their family. She also reclaimed a lost part of her own family. She wrote the news of her engagement, and of her rupture with Lady Catherine, to her cousins, Mr Darcy and Colonel Fitzwilliam—from whom she had been for some time estranged, owing to their own quarrels with her mother— and received in reply messages of congratulation, and assurances of friendship from them both. The Fitzwilliams were unable to attend Anne's wedding, but forwarded their hearty good wishes by the post. The Darcys travelled all the way from Derbyshire with their young daughter, Jane, and Mr Darcy's sister Georgiana, to be present at the marriage; and, as Mr and Mrs Darcy were both greatly pleased by what they saw of Captain Turner during their stay in Hampshire, they invited the newlyweds to return the favour by paying a long visit to Pemberley, whenever a break in the captain's duties would permit them to make the journey.

If, beyond those inescapable anxieties which had their origin in the perils of her husband's profession, Anne had any sorrows to becloud her newfound joy, one might be found in the loss of Charlotte Collins, who could not oppose the joint commands of Mr Collins and Lady Catherine to renounce her friendship. Indeed Charlotte's own feelings about the marriage were somewhat ambivalent. She liked Captain Turner, and could even believe his choice of Anne de Bourgh to be a disinterested one—as disinterested, that is, as the choice of a man who weds an heiress may ever be supposed to be. But for Anne de Bourgh to relinquish all the wealth and ease of Rosings to marry a man, however amiable, of small fortune and uncertain prospects, was an excess of sentiment which the pragmatic Mrs Collins could hardly comprehend. She was sorry, nevertheless, to be once more thrown back upon the exclusive society of Mr Collins and Lady Catherine, and keenly missed the pleasant and rational conversation which her intimacy with Anne had afforded her. She did hear news of her from time to time, however, through her friend Mrs Darcy (the former Miss Bennet); and she ventured to indulge a hope that, some time hence, her ladyship's resentment would abate, and she would again receive Anne as her daughter. That hope was strengthened when Lady Catherine—perhaps finding solitude less to her taste than she had expected, with only the unrelieved devotion of Mr Collins to make up for the loss of her child— grudgingly yielded to Mr Darcy's overtures of reconciliation, and admitted him once again to the privilege of claiming her as a relation. With her nephew's influence exerted in Anne's behalf—and perhaps the birth of a grandchild to reawaken her parental feelings—there was every reason to anticipate an eventual relenting on Lady Catherine's side; and Charlotte could not doubt but that any rapprochement would be welcomed on Anne's.

It is not known for certain what fate finally befell the Wynnewoods; but at one time a rumour was circulated in their former neighbourhood of Cumberland (as Mrs Goulding heard from her sister, and subsequently related to Lady Lucas, who wrote of it to Mrs Collins) that, after leaving Bath, the family fled to the continent, eventually making their way to the spa town of Karlsbad. There, according to report, George Wynnewood met and married a rich spinster twenty years his senior; and his sister Louisa soon afterward caught the fancy of an elderly Austrian count, who was so kind and obliging a husband as to drop dead during the honeymoon, leaving her thereby a very wealthy, and a very merry widow.

Anne de Bourgh married later in life than most; but her married life was happier than most as well. She never regretted having relinquished the fortune and position to which she was born: for she had acquired in their stead a husband for whom she felt both tenderness and esteem; and the captain's affection for her never diminished or varied. I can offer no better proof of the enduring strength of their mutual love than this: that though, in the world's judgment, Anne Turner was always reckoned a plain woman, in her husband's eyes she grew more beautiful with every passing year; and, though common opinion pronounced Samuel Turner to be rather an ill-favoured gentleman, in his wife's estimation he was always the handsomest man in any company.

~Finis~

End Notes

Holt's Elixir (Chapter 1)
In 1815, Holt's Elixir was still a popular tonic, and in high repute. It was not until 1832, after the death of Mr Holt, that his son Felix put an end to the manufacture and sale of the quack medicines by which his father had once earned a comfortable profit.

Hit-and-run driver (Chapter 2)
The driver of the carriage which flattened her ladyship has never been positively identified; however, some witnesses at the scene, noting the conspicuous style of the driver's attire, as well as his scandalous disregard for the public safety, believe the culprit to have been a gentleman by the name of Thorpe.

Man who shoots off his gun (Chapter 7)
See footnote for Chapter 2 above, Hit-and-run driver.

Boggley-Wollah (Chapter 16)
A country in the Bengal region of India, 'situated in a fine, lonely, marshy, jungly district, famous for snipe-shooting, and where not unfrequently you may flush a tiger'. (W.M. Thackeray)